STRIKE FOR A KINGDOM

Angela V. John is Professor of History at the University of Greenwich and originally from Port Talbot. Her publications include: (with Revel Guest) *Lady Charlotte. A Biography of the Nineteenth Century*, Weidenfeld & Nicolson, 1989 and editing *Our Mothers' Land. Chapters in Welsh Women's History, 1830-1939*, University of Wales Press, 1991. She is currently completing her eighth book, *Henry W. Nevinson. War, Journalism and Justice*. She knew Menna Gallie well.

STRIKE FOR
A KINGDOM

by

MENNA GALLIE

With an introduction
by
Angela V. John

HONNO CLASSICS

Published by Honno
'Alisa Craig', Heol y Cawl, Dinas Powys
South Glamorgan, Wales, CF6 4AH

First published in England by Victor Gollancz Ltd., in 1959
This edition © Honno Ltd 2003

© *Menna Gallie 1959*
© *Introduction Angela V. John 2003*

NOTE
All the characters in this book are fictitious

British Library Cataloguing in Publication Data

With thanks to Annest Wiliam

ISBN 1 870206 58 4

Published with the financial support of the Arts Council of Wales

Cover image of Menna Gallie courtesy of Annest Wiliam

Cover design by Chris Lee Design

Typeset and printed in Wales by Gwasg Dinefwr, Llandybïe

Introduction

ANGELA V. JOHN

In the summer of 1926 Menna Humphreys was six. Unlike most of her friends in the Swansea Valley village of Ystradgynlais, her father was not a collier on strike but a craftsman. Each Sunday he ritualistically divided a bar of chocolate between his three daughters, Nansi, Pegi and Menna, meticulously measuring out their portions with his carpenter's ruler. One particular week Menna stood outside her front door to savour her treat on her own. Just as she was smoothing out the empty wrapper, a little girl who had been intently watching her from a distance came up and whispered, 'Can I have the smell of the paper?' In later years Menna Gallie would claim that it was this pitiful request which prompted her to write *Strike for a Kingdom*, her first novel. Whether or not this was so – she was a consummate teller of stories who could always transform retrospectively even the most humdrum event into a drama – the effect of the General Strike on her local community, and thus on the young Menna, was a lasting one.

Menna Gallie was from a Welsh-speaking, socialist background. Her father was a north-Walian but her mother was local, one of nine children, eight of whom lived within two miles of each other. In this extended family 'aunts stood around us like the Druid's stones'. When the wireless came, her eldest aunt would elect to listen to the fatstock prices in Welsh rather than hear even a religious service in English. Her maternal grandfather, a colliery checkweighman who also ran a small farm, had helped found the Labour Representation Committee in south Wales. Keir Hardie had stayed at her grandparents' house and her monoglot grandmother proudly claimed to have two sentences of English: 'I like ice cream' and 'Keir Hardie called me Comrade'. Menna Gallie's mother became secretary of the local women's section of the Labour Party though her roots lay in the Independent Labour Party. The Humphreys children sang Welsh hymns at the Congregational chapel and eisteddfodau but they also sang 'God Save the People' at home. Menna Gallie remained a lifelong Labour Party activist, maintaining that she was 'not much of an "-ist" except that I'm a Socialist'.

Growing up in Ystradgynlais and Creunant (in the Dulais valley), then studying for an English degree at Swansea University, it is hardly surprising that Menna Gallie set *Strike for a Kingdom* (1959) and *The Small Mine* (1962) in a Welsh mining village. She named it Cilhendre. *The Small Mine* explores the time when the new National Coal Board coexisted cheek-by-jowl with the many small, private drift mines. Yet critical of the 'sociology and sentimentality' to which mining communities were continually subjected, she challenged (though also sometimes unconsciously reinforced) the stereotypical imagery of the mining village. However, only two of her six novels were actually set in the valleys communities she knew best even though two others were about Welsh people. Her last novel, as yet published only in America, *In These Promiscuous Parts* (1986), is located in north Pembrokeshire where she spent her last years (for Trenewydd read Newport/Trefdraeth). She also wrote a booklet about the folklore of this part of Pembrokeshire, *Little England's Other Half* (1974). In 1973 her translation of Caradog Prichard's sombre novel *Un Nos Ola Leuad* appeared, entitled *Full Moon*.

Strike for a Kingdom was hidden away for two years in a drawer before it saw the light of day. When Menna Gallie was eventually persuaded to retrieve it, the manuscript was immediately accepted by the respected left-wing publisher Victor Gollancz. Pronounced 'fresh and beguiling' by the *Times Literary Supplement*, it was well reviewed and Gollancz went on to publish five of her six novels. Her fiction also appeared in America. There she initially received greater acclaim than in the UK, her popularity perhaps prompted in part by comparisons her early critics made with the work of Dylan Thomas. *Strike for a Kingdom* was declared to be 'a poet's novel' despite being partly a 'whodunnit'.

Now Menna Gallie is at last receiving here the critical acclaim she deserves. Two of her novels have already been reprinted as Honno Classics, she features in Honno's anthology of women's lives in the south Wales valleys in the inter-war period, *Struggle or Starve* and her work is being dramatised for radio and stage.

Menna Gallie's Cilhendre stories were not written in Wales. Here she was creating what seems to have become a pattern for her fiction: experiencing a community at first-hand but delaying writing about it until her thoughts had gestated for some time and she had moved on to a new place. Thus *Strike for a Kingdom* was actually written in Ulster, as was her second novel, *Man's Desiring* (1960). In 1940 she had married, just four days before he went off to the army, a philosophy lecturer at Swansea, a Scot called Bryce Gallie. *Man's Desiring*, with hints of Kingsley Amis's better-known *Lucky Jim*, concerns a Welsh working-class lad who tries to make it at an English university. It is based on the time the Gallies spent at Keele, where Bryce Gallie was appointed the first Professor of Philosophy.

Her tragi-comedy, *You're Welcome to Ulster!* (1970) was written in Cambridge. The experience of being a don's wife at Peterhouse (Bryce Gallie held the Chair of Political Science at Cambridge between 1967 and 1978) was not one Menna

Gallie relished. She had far preferred the years in Northern Ireland where her son and daughter had grown up. Significantly, there is no novel about the Cambridge years. Yet in *Travels with a Duchess* (1968), the story of two middle-aged women shedding inhibitions on a holiday in 1960s Yugoslavia, she describes how the academic wife tends to look a decade older than her husband, feeling the strain of being 'the little handmaiden, helpmate, slave, they get to look like caricatures of denial'. Cambridge brought out most keenly her innate defence of women's rights in the face of institutional denial.

Yet Menna Gallie was wary of the label 'feminist'. In 1985, five years before her death at the age of seventy, she gave a talk at Onllwyn Miners' Welfare Hall in the Dulais Valley, addressing an audience of academics interested in Welsh women's history and miners' wives who had been making some of that history during the recent strike. She carefully denied that she was a feminist. White-haired and crippled with arthritis, she looked deceptively frail. Yet she always delighted in provoking, in shocking, in protesting. She spoke for over an hour, telling stories about her life, her practice and attitudes, palpably belying her verbal protestations.

Strike for a Kingdom does not open with a chocolate wrapper but it does have little girls skipping to a rhyme about chewing gum made of wax. And it is set at the time of the protracted miners' Lock Out which followed the short-lived General Strike of May 1926. August has arrived and the Carnival is going ahead. Organised by the strike committee, it enables the community to show that it can come together despite, or because of, adversity. The first prize for fancy dress (owing much to the ingenuity and sewing of mothers) is a half-pound bar of Cadbury's.

We are first shown Cilhendre through the eyes of a small,

awkward girl. But the perspective soon shifts. The heightened atmosphere of a carnival is a common fictional device for revealing more sinister undertones. And so it proves here with the discovery of the corpse of the colliery manager. Murder in their midst pushes loyalty to extremes. And this is a novel essentially concerned with loyalties, both to the cause and to the community. Men and women provide false alibis to protect their own. Inspector Evans lacks sympathy with the striking miners so elides their actions with (literally) more deadly deeds. He is not a local man but he is Welsh and disloyal to his own roots, able to speak the language but, like a lot of social climbers then and for some decades after, 'preferred not to let it be known that he suffered from this disability'.

Competing loyalties are tearing apart the novel's most interesting character: D. J. Williams, a gentle man, poet-collier on strike and magistrate. *Strike for a Kingdom* is prefaced with the standard statement that 'All the characters in this book are fictitious'. But its author later explained that D.J. was based on her Uncle William, commonly known as W.R. W. R. Williams had been a Ruskin student, was a striking miner, a poet, magistrate and became a Labour County Councillor.

The use of the initials D.J. may have signified both a surplus of Williamses in the community and the character's conflicting loyalties: D.J. the miners' butty is also the J.P., the dispenser of justice. But whose justice and where does he stand? At one moment we see him marching with the strikers to the coal owner's house and, after an episode which suggests the ineptitude of the local constabulary rather than the sort of drama found in Zola's *Germinal*, he is placed in the police cells in Neath for the night. But when Inspector Evans (who has never heard of the modern authors in D.J.'s bookcase) brings him summonses to sign, D.J. does so 'like Judas Iscariot'.

The difficulties facing working class magistrates and the dilemma of a class conscious collier who genuinely values peaceful persuasion – 'as usual with D.J., wisdom prevailed' – are finely balanced here. Interestingly, in a world associated with 'macho' values and proving manliness, Menna Gallie chooses to make her hero, as his mam observes, highly sensitive.

By using deft thumb-nail sketches of the miners, Menna Gallie ensures that they are all individuals and not an undifferentiated mass. At the same time she is able, in a few words, to convey both rich humour and deep anger. Take, for example, Tommy Davies who was sitting across the street: 'a nice quiet chap. He was used to sitting; he'd been on the Compensation for months before the Strike. Christ, he could cough'.

Men and women in Cilhendre appear to inhabit separate worlds. The colliers, used to working together, now gather around the coal tips as their alternative to a workplace. The women talk together and it is interesting to note that they know about the murder before the chairman of the strike committee. This is not an industrial novel wound round close-knit family units as in Gwyn Jones's novel of the General Strike, *Times Like These*, set in a south Wales valleys community further east. There are some very lonely people in Cilhendre trapped within marriages and homes. Next door to D.J. live Gethin, his mother and his dying sister Gwen. Especially tragic is Jess Jeffries who had 'obliged for the manager' in order to feed her family and whose 'whorin'' was condoned by her husband 'when we're hungry, but by Christ, I'll belt you if you don't mind your words'. What Jess now fears most is being denounced from the pulpit. Here Menna Gallie reveals the less compassionate sides of faith, family and community.

Inspector Evans is the sort of man who 'shouts for his

breakfast'. At times he and his side-kick, P.C. Thomas, seem almost pantomimic. Evans is shown up by the generosity of Williams the Road and his large family who overwhelm the policemen with gifts of fruit and veg., in one of the few scenes depicting family life as a positive, if somewhat frenetic, experience. But this follows their visit to a farmer's widow who had been so pestered by men that she now threatens them all with a rifle.

Alongside the tale of murder runs another tragic death. The body of a still-born baby is found close by. Without dwelling on it, Menna Gallie suggests the shame of being an unmarried mother at this time and there is a hint of darker secrets.

Strike for a Kingdom is not as focused on women's lives as *The Small Mine* and *Travels with a Duchess*. It even uses what today seem like politically incorrect similes such as 'Like a nosy old woman'. Yet, as with Menna Gallie's repudiation of the trappings of modern feminism, beneath the surface is an empathy with the perspectives of her female characters.

Note her depiction of the upper-middle class manager's wife. A woman 'Repressed by good manners, she was like a grate decorated with a paper fan, never meant for a fire' but when she hears about the dead baby, gender transcends class and she expresses a compassion which she has not evinced for her murdered husband. This is beyond the comprehension of Inspector Evans who, for once, finds himself confused and redundant: 'The Inspector got up, and for the first time in his life left some whiskey in the bottom of his glass. He was moved'.

Strike for a Kingdom is good value. Menna Gallie gives us a detective story and a compassionate novel of a troubled Welsh mining valley, conjuring up a vivid sense of time and place. She also provides a witty and wonderfully observed cameo of social behaviour.

CHAPTER 1

"Chewing-gum, chewing-gum ma-ade of wax,
Brought me to my grave at last.
High upon the mántelpiece,
There you'll find a báll of grease,
Shining like a thrípenny piece
And out goes she."

Six or seven small girls were skipping with a long rope held
across the August road. One of the children, holding the far
end of the rope, stood almost inside a dusty hawthorn hedge,
while the other stood on the doorstep of "Cartref" a small
semi-detached house standing at the end of Cilhendre village
street. As the rope was turned, heavy and rhythmic, the other
children jumped into the twirl of it and chanted,

"Chewing-gum, chewing-gum ma-ade of wax."

The art was to keep skipping until the end of the stanza
and then to leap gracefully away without disturbing the
rhythm of the rope. Most of the little bouncing girls succeeded, but one hung back to the very end of the line and
when at last it was inevitably her turn, she set her projecting
teeth well into her lower lip, blushed, prayed and doggedly
ran at the rope. She jumped up, far too high, far too deter-
mined, and at once tangled her feet and long doe's legs and
stopped the rope.

In silent acceptance of what having Nan in the skipping
always meant, the children changed the turners and started
again.

"The wind, the wind blows high,
The rain comes scattering from the sky;"

while Nan, her faith in God once more destroyed, leaned on the window-sill of Cartref. There she was joined by Blodwen Bevan, her friend, whom she hated almost as much at the moment, as she hated God.

Blodwen was full of the pursed-in confidence of an elderly gossip. "My mother said Gwen Evans in there is very bad in bed and sure to die."

"Will they have a funeral?" Nan said, looking into the setting sun, away from the skipping.

"Yes, sure to be. We had a lovely funeral, remember, when Uncle Willie died. I had one of the ribbons off a wreath for Sunday. Sitting on the stairs we were to hear the singing and Mammy was crying out loud. And after, we had a big tea with cook-'am. Have you ever been to a funeral, Nan?"

"No."

"Come you, I expect you'll have one. Have you got anybody old?"

"I don't know."

"Of course you have. You got your Grannie."

"My Grannie can't have a funeral."

"Why?"

"Well, she's my Grannie that's why." Nan was gripped by her terrible despair which was becoming almost habitual; she wanted to cry, from the soles of her feet. She knew they'd never have a funeral or anything unless perhaps she died, but then she wouldn't have a ribbon. But they might all be nicer to her if she did die, if only for a little while.

"Are you going to the Carnival, Nan?"

"I 'spect so."

"What are you going as, then? You won't be a fairy for sure, nor a bride. Your teeth spoils you, don't they? P'raps they'll fall out. Our Dai's did."

"No. They won't, they're my second teeth and they feel strong, like two big rocks. There's not much chance – unless I can get knocked down by a bike."

"Well, I'm going like a fairy, whatever. I got a wand too with a star on it."

Nan looked at Blodwen with desperate, despairing envy, at her ringlets, made every night with rags, at her doll's eyes that looked like china, at her sharp, small, pointed teeth that hid properly behind her lip. Nan's eyes, that her mother called "her redeeming feature," filled with ever ready tears and went pink around the rims as Blodwen pushed herself off the window-sill and jumped to take her turn in the skipping. Nan turned her head to follow the pattern in the lace curtains behind her and pretended not to notice when it was her turn to skip.

She pushed her tears away with her fist when her face was out of sight and decided to give God another chance. Tomorrow, before anyone at home could find her and shake their heads over her, she would look for a good hiding-place, somewhere nice and light, and if God didn't let them find her before the Carnival, she'd give Him one more try. Before she had to face the indignity of that rope again, a man came out of Cartref and asked the little girls, in a funny, choking voice, if they'd go and play somewhere else because they were making a bit too much noise for Gwen. The owner of the rope, Blodwen of course, quickly lapped it around her middle.

"All right, Mr. Evans. We was going home. Our Mammy will be shoutin' for me. Carnival tomorrow, must have a bath and go to bed early tonight."

The shrill children went their separate ways. Nan and Blodwen, who were neighbours, went together and Nan announced that she was going to the Carnival dressed as a queen, that they had a real queen's dress in their house and

a real gold crown and she would wear it tomorrow. She
didn't for a moment expect Blodwen to believe her, but her
lies, as she consciously thought of them, came pouring out
of her mind as though of their own volition. She was not
aware of thinking them before they were out, and was sometimes amazed herself by the glories of her lies. They arrived
at their doors, and as Blodwen called, "See you tomorrow,"
Nan went on with her plans. She went into her own house,
sulky and guilty and resentful, unable to accept the love and
welcome there because she mistrusted it all. Who could love
her with those teeth? She sought revenge in impertinence
and sulks and went to bed in disgrace.

CHAPTER 2

From the top of the tips Cilhendre was a little huddle of pigeon-coloured houses following the curves of the River Tawe, which plaited its way among them, with the road and railway for company. The sun polished the walls of the houses. They were built of river stones, lavender grey, cloud grey, sea grey, pink and purple. One side of the valley faced the sun and was golden and pink in the warmth. The hills on the other side were in deep shadow, deeply blue.

Up on the tips there were clusters of people, with bags and sacks, picking bits of coal. On the rowdy tip, they shouted and teased, strikers on holiday, mufflers and flat caps, working boots and fine, new, ladies' hands. The strike began in May and they'd been hungry many times since, but this was August and Carnival, Carnival Wednesday after August Monday, and their bellies were full of Soup Kitchen dinner.

"Oi, Joe, did you go on your fox-hunt last night, boy?" a fat man like a Royal Baby asked Joe Everynight, who was the father of twelve children.

"No, he went up with the blinds, mun."

"Yes I did then; we went up the Drym, see. Me and the boys."

"Did you take the missis?"

"Not up the Drym, mun; too many gnats."

"Shut up now, boys bach, let me tell you about the fox-'unt. You know that bit of a wood by Tynewydd, don't you? Well, we was hidin' in by there, see – waitin' for the old boy. Will Swank was with us, braggin' about the time he'd seen a real 'unt, with horses and all. Smellin' of scenty soap he was and we was havin' a smoke and talkin' quiet. Lewis Baboon was on the watch and he saw the fox comin', mun, nippin' down the hill, fast as a bloody fairy. Old Lewis didn't want foxy to know we was after 'im, and shouts out, for us to hear, F-O-X, thinking the poor bloody old fox couldn't read. Old foxy didn't think much of readin' lessons and he was away like a bullet. I didn't have a chance, mun. But we'll get him yet, come you, schoolin' and all."

"You won't go after him tonight, whatever."

"Diawl no, boyo, I wouldn't miss the march tonight, not for a night with a tart from Cardiff."

"Joe, did you hear the latest about old Baldwin? They say, that old Mrs. Baldwin was addressin' a meeting of women Conservatives, the bloody leeches, and talkin' about the glories of England and the Empiahh" – the revolutionary struck a dramatic pose, and set a face upon the sunny tips – "She's supposed to have said, 'As we married women unfortunately know, there are certain aspects of marriage at which a gentlewoman shudders, but, ladies, I find that it is possible to live out these times if one sets one's teeth and thinks of ENGLAND!'"

In the laughter and sympathy for any man with such a wife, D. J. Williams, one of the coal pickers, who was a Justice of Peace and a poet, realised that it was time he went home to tidy up for the Carnival. He was one of the Carnival judges. He stretched his backbone and straightened his cap and took a last sly look at the village below him. He picked up his sack, half filled with poor coal and slack.

"So long, boys. I'll have to be going. Got to shave and tidy up. See you in the Carnival, no doubt."

"So long, D.J. So long, now."

"Oi, D.J., remember to give the prize to our Gwyneth."

"What is she going as? Hope of the Side? The baby will go as a ball, p'raps."

The Justice, a peace-loving, quiet man, slithered and

stumbled down, sliding on his backside sometimes like a boy. The sun was warm on his dirty face and he breathed as deep as his cough would let him – enjoying his freedom, a middle-aged truant out in the light, in the day. He walked home through his village that was his birthplace, his world. As the sun warmed his back through his working clothes, bits and words of poetry slipped like beads through his mind. He had been unable to sleep the previous night. He was worried about the Strike and the strikers and whether tonight's march was wise or not. He had gone for a walk in the small hours and had been soothed by the mountains and the dark and the poems he had been able to remember. He walked down the village street, his small sack pulling him down a little on one side. Sometimes he coughed harshly. His face was hollowed at the cheeks, but he had a new colour from the sunshine. His eyes were deep blue and laughter-wrinkled at the corners.

His mother kept house for D.J. A kindly, amused, dignified woman, still beautiful, still wearing the fashions of the 1890s, the dignity of long skirts, small waist, high collar and white upswept hair. Her English was limited but her Welsh was lyrical, biblical, rich with unconscious metaphor.

She accepted his burden of coal with her smile and poured warm water into the zinc bath she had set before the fireplace. While he washed clean like a collier, she boiled an egg for him, cut his bread and butter and made his tea. He shaved in the back kitchen when his meal was over and then put on his navy blue suit over his striped flannel shirt and "sham-front". When Davy was ready his mother brushed his suit and said, "Remember all the things that make you laugh, Davy bach, and keep them for me." She would not go to the Carnival. It was a question of what was fitting.

Jack Look-Out, another collier, came down from the tips. He was in what his wife described as one of his "nasty" moods. Silent and irritable and bitter. It was a long time since he had had a few drinks and he was always difficult when he wanted beer. Sarah, his wife, made a cup of tea for him and some bread and dripping. He ate without a word and she sat quiet, like a ferret.

There was a knock at the door and a woman put her head round.

"Are you in, Sarah?"

"Yes, come on you, Doris."

"Oh, having food, is it? Sorry to upset you. I only came to ask if you was going to the Carnival."

"Yes, I think I'll go. Something to do like."

"Wat'll you wear, then?"

"She's going like Lady Godiva, didn't you know? I won't have to bloody change. I'll go like a bloody scarecrow, just like I am." Jack got up from the dark corner between the fireplace and the window and spat straight into the grate."See the coal in it? In the spit I mean, not the bloody grate." He shambled out in stockinged feet to sit on his haunches at his front door. He sat in the sun, the chronic bitterness of him belching up with the taste of bread and dripping.

Across the street Tommy Davies was sitting, a nice quiet chap. He was used to sitting; he'd been on the Compensation for months before the Strike. Christ, he could cough.

"Lovely day, Jack."

"Aye."

"Sun's shining nice for the Carnival."

"Aye. Shining like a dog's balls."

"Are you going?"

"To make a bloody fool of myself for a pack of women? No fear, boyo."

"Come on, now, it's a bit of sport. The kids love it. It's hard on them just now."

The two women came out of the house and stood together at the front door; crinkling their eyes up in the sun, enjoying the warmth of gossip, shared complaints and sunshine. Sarah was thin, scraggy, red-nosed, getting on for forty; she wore a black serviceable pinafore over an old green jumper, pinned at the neck – the grimy neck that showed her age. Her hair was still black, still stringy, her eyes were black too and would have been stringy if they could. She had the knack of easy crying, so useful when the money had all been spent.

She stood there in the sunshine, cleaning her false teeth with her tongue, pushing them half out of her mouth to explore the crevices in the plate. Her husband watched her and again he wondered at himself that he had been brought to marry her. The Family Way. That's what did it; the bloody fool he'd been too. Taken in. There never was a child. He spat again. Tasted the dripping.

"So long, then," Doris muttered, reluctant to leave the company, lazy, shiftless.

"So long." They watched her walking up the narrow street, on the warm side of the road, her buttocks wobbling, her feet turning over her heels, the fairish hair bouncing on the back of her neck in a bundle of curlers. Jack would have liked to feel a creep of desire for her in the sun there, but you can't do much on strike pay. Dripping doesn't go far enough.

"Are you turning out today, Tommy?"

"Yes, Sarah. I've had an idea. Can't sleep much these nights somehow and I got a good idea in bed. I've collected all the old matches I could find about the place and I've sewed them on my old working clothes. I'm going to have a placard saying 'No more Strikes'. None in the matches, see, and no more for me, not with this old chest I got by here."

"Well, there's clever for you. Real smart. Why don't you think of something, our Jack; you fancy yourself enough?"

Jack spat again. "Carnival, my arse."

"Well, there's no need to use language, whatever." And Sarah went into her witch's house and closed the door on the sun that showed up the dirt.

The men sat on in silence. Jack bit his nails clean, itching for a cigarette. He linked his hands together, pressing them down till the knuckles cracked. He got up and crossed the road to sit beside Tommy.

"Saw the old bugger last night. He came down here from you-know-where just after eleven. Been for a bit with Jess. Where Elwyn was I don't know. Out poachin' p'raps. Why the hell he don't see what's under his nose beats me."

"Maybe he don't want to see. I expect Dai Bloomers gives her a few quid for it and it helps to feed the kids. Elwyn thinks a lot of those kids of his."

"If they are his."

"Course they're his. They were born before Dai B. ever came to Cilhendre. I wonder what his wife thinks? Does she know? They tell me she's very good to those two girls who work in the house and she's been a real Christian to that poor Gwen Evans, Gerwin's sister."

"She could keep her bloody charity if they was my girls. She gets it off of our backs in the first place. I didn't half tell old Bloomers last night. He ran flat into me, see, by here in the street. Laugh! There was a good moon, see, and he was walking quiet, close to the houses for a bit of shadow. I'd been round the backs and came round the corner sudden. When he saw me I thought he'd have to change his trousers, aye. I said, all polite and la-di-da, 'Good night, Mr. Nixon. Nice night for a bit of all right, isn't it?'

"'Oh,' he said, trying to be offhand, like Sarah when the Insurance man caught her hidin' behind the door, pretendin' to be out, 'Oh, good night, Jack' – Jack, mind you, not you lazy rodney like he called me underground – 'I've been for a bit of a walk,' he says. 'I can't sleep very well these warm nights. Worrying times for us all.' And he put his hand in his pocket, mun, and offered me half a crown hush-money – half a crown, mind you. I was dyin' to take it too – five bloody pints – but I says, 'No, thanks, Mr. Bloomers, give it to Jess.' And he turns sharp and off down the road like a ha-penny squib."

They laughed together until Tommy started to cough again and Jack got up, shamed by the coughing and the spitting. With a nod of his head he crossed the road back to his own house. He went through the house and into the back yard. He sat on the wall, resting his back on the tarred, corrugated iron shed which felt like a radiator and reminded him of school. He stared at the fine grey stones that paved the yard and at the tap in the corner. He was remembering last night again. The joke was on himself now, because he remembered that last night he had prayed, without thinking. It was the first time that he had prayed for years; it had been a short little prayer, "Christ, mun, try and keep it quiet, will you?" He had gone to bed then. He had a quick vision of himself as he must have looked getting in beside Sarah in his pants and shirt. His black and calloused knees had shown through the holes in his tight, shrunken once-white pants, and he knew that the seat of them hung slack where a patch on the behind had not shrunk. He saw their bed, brass and creaking like a tramcar, and himself finding the grooves in the flock that fitted his large, strong body. The bed had been warm with the smell of the two of them and Sarah was asleep on the other side. Her teeth had grinned at him, where they had slipped from under the pillow, and in the grey room, full of bed, he'd looked at her, ugly, thin, a chest like fried eggs, she had no business in a bed. "You poor bugger," he'd said quietly.

Jess, who obliged for the manager, Mr. Nixon, Mr. Dai Bloomers, was a dark, stoutish woman in her late thirties. She was generous, soft-fleshed, big-bosomed, big-buttocked, kindly and as sentimental as Danny Boy. She would lend you the last thing in her house, even when it wasn't hers to lend.

She was kind to the manager in just the same way as she was kind to all the kids in the street. There was no nonsense about old love, but it was a pity for the poor man and she liked to do a favour when she could. The money was lovely for the children and perhaps Elwyn would never find out.

Her children were three little girls, dark like their mother, but tall and thin and growing fast. She delighted in dressing them alike and in tying coloured ribbons in their hair, the cheeky robins. They were going to the Carnival in the Welsh costumes they had had for last St. David's Day Eisteddfod. The frills under the tall black hats were white and crinkly around their robin faces. Red flannel petticoats and black-and-white shawls were dashing, like soldiers, but itched like a haystack. Already the children were scratching and wriggling and sweating in their hottest-day flannel. But that was like Jess, she never saw further than red flannel and looking nice.

She fed her itching daughters and Elwyn her husband, and helped him, with brown boot polish, to become a Red Indian in sacks. When they were turned out to her satisfaction she went upstairs, to dress herself while they waited for her. She put on her white best blouse and a navy blue serge suit, tight across the chest, which changed her lovely loose breasts into a kind of fat pin-cushion. She came downstairs trim and tidy with her stays creaking like a bed, and was ready to go to watch the Carnival.

CHAPTER 3

The Miners' Strike in 1926 lasted from May until December. Then the cold beat them. They came out demanding an increase in the minimum wage and the eventual nationalisation of the industry. They were not trouble makers for the fun of it, they were not Marxists out to destroy Capitalism; they did not think of themselves as "one of the Factors of Production", but they felt they were poor devils having a raw deal and they had had enough. Their strike, for most of them, had little to do with economic theory. They were sick of working underground in the dark, getting silicosis and accidents galore for two quid a week – and this only for the lucky ones who were at work. On the dole a single man got seventeen bob a week. This was a strike of Oliver Twists and the Owners had much in common with the Beadle.

When D. J. Williams left his home he stepped into the chaos of dress rehearsal; clowns and gypsies, fairies and beggars, crinoline ladies, ministers, wedding parties, negro minstrels, Red Indians, all wearing Cilhendre faces, looking foolish and feeling ridiculous, the courage of their homes melting like the blacking on their faces and running down in sweat between their legs.

They went down to the field in shy little clusters, trying to hide, waiting for the procession and the crowd to bind them, to dissolve them and submerge their identities. They straggled into the field and formed an untidy queue near the judges' table which had stood small and lonely in the middle of the big field. Confidence began to seep back as they saw their neighbours looking even more foolish than they felt themselves, and, suddenly, the Carnival was on. It was officially opened with a speech given by the oldest member of the Strike Committee. He was sixty-nine and still a collier, his face and hands very scarred and one eye was pulled badly out of shape. Old Eye was no Lloyd George, no orator, but miners have a touching faith in the Seniority Rule.

"Comrades," he began, "Comrades bach, we have gathered here today to have a carnival. It is a good idea to have a bit of a spree, like, to cheer us up in these unhappy times. But, comrades, they are good times too because they are showing that we are comrades, that we are one behind the other against those up by there who have brought us to this pass. All my life I have been a Trade Union and a Co-op and I am proud to say it. We will have wonderful today again and now if you please we will sing all together 'Are we down-hearted?' No, Comrades, No!"

There was a cheer for Eye and then, with voices that moved your bowels and made the goose-flesh creep up your arms, the crowd sang the song of the defeated, "Are we down-hearted? Oh, no, no." Then, intoxicated with their own splendid sounds and led by a tenor who "has long since drunk himself to death", they sang softly a local parody of "When it's Springtime in the Rockies" – "When it's Spring-time in the Rhondda and the men are on the dole." They followed this, because it was a day for the children too, with

> "Rock-a-bye baby on the tree top,
> When you grow up you'll work in a shop,
> When you get married your wife will work too,
> Just for the rich to have nothing to do."

Not bitterly, just singing, because they were in a crowd, holiday colliers.

In a wave of catcalls and comments the Strike Committee men tried to form the procession up in twos: tutting and fussing and shouting orders to which nobody listened. At last they managed to get the smallest ones, two fairies in white and tinsel, to the front and the rowdy Red Indian jazz band at the back. The smallest fairy was already tired and sticky and trailed her curtain-rod wand in the dust. The mothers of the fairies hurried up to take their hands and give them courage. Next to the fairies were Joe Everynight's twelve children, all dressed in flour sacks, Spiller's Fine Ground. The smallest child's sack trailed to the ground and the sack of the eldest one scarcely covered her bottom. This one wore a card on her back "The Bread Line". Their mother twitched them tidy.

Jack Look-Out was a great success at the Carnival. He had thrown off his earlier depression and was a little drunk. He had dressed in a borrowed tweed suit and had pushed the trouser legs into his socks to make thin plus-fours. He carried a cane and wore a tweed cap, snappy, at an angle. Arm in arm with him walked one of his drinking cronies, a bookie's runner, in a makeshift policeman's uniform. The runner's face was painted bright red with post office ink and he wore a white cotton-wool moustache. He did look something like the Police Inspector, the Manager's friend. On their backs their cards read "Birds of a Feather".

The fattest man in Cilhendre, Moc Cow-and-Gate, the Royal Baby, was undressed in a small raffia skirt hung just below his deep, dimpling navel. Under this he paraded a large pair of knickers, directoire style. The rest of him was covered with Zebo, and he glistened in the sun like Sunday shoes. He wore a necklace of four large bones, stolen from some unfortunate dog. He carried a wooden spear with which he made terrifying darts at the other characters. That finished the second fairy, Blodwen, who promptly wet her knickers and had to go home to have them changed.

There were two football teams dressed like young ladies

in feather boas and hats and skirts and stockings that always needed hoisting up so that suspenders and underwear could be revealed. The Impossibles and The Improbables. They upset the procession by kicking balls about, trying to undress each other and clanging the saucepans that they carried.

In the end the Committee men gave up trying to tidy them and retired, hurt, to their table. The Red Indians started playing "Sospan Fach" on their horrible whistles called gazooks. This set feet on edge and off they went, round the field and out through the gate.

"Oo! look at our Evan. He's got my best blouse on, he'll have it when I catch him . . ."

"Duw Mawr? look at the hair on Dai Yankie's legs. Like goin' out with a bear . . ."

"Our Mam, look, Gethin is using language on his back – he's got bum on his back, Mam, bum, bum, bum . . ."

"Shut up. For shame on you! 'Halleluia, I'm a bum.' Oh! there's rude – W'at's he want that for, Jinny?"

"Well! Drop dead. Cow-and-Gate is showing his belly-button . . . Drat this dog, he's after the bones. Down, Fido, down."

"Hoi, Willy, your front is slipping. They're by your waist boy. Yes, take them out to play football, that's better."

"There's shameful, how some women can I don't know."

"You'll never have another job in Cilhendre, Jack. You've had your cards, boy."

"Down, Fido. That's not the manager, don't bite him, boy."

"Duw! Mrs. Everynight makes a hell of a lot of bread. I can see Gwyneth's behind in that sack. Fair play, too."

"Aw! look at Jess's three in all that flannel. Come you love, take your shawl off and carry it."

"No. My mother said to wear it."

"Are you hot?"

"Boiling."

"Pity. Never mind, p'raps you'll win."

"W'at's the prizes, Jinny?"

"Watkins the Grocer gave a few bags of sweets, for the kids, I heard, and there's pounds of sugar for the big ones."

"Well, did you ever! There's Twm the Singing with those Indians, and him a deacon. W'at ever next, girl?"

As they passed through the gates of the Welfare Field, Jim Jesus was standing on a kitchen chair, preaching. He preached against carnivals, against football, against the pictures, against being happy and laughing and smoking cigarettes. He kept making gestures with his arms as though he were throwing something far out. He was "throwing out the life-line, some-one is drifting away." Nobody felt inclined to catch it that afternoon and the procession went on, singing now, as a tribute to Jim "Jesus knows all about my troubles".

Somewhere in the rout dragged a little daunted girl whose faith had been destroyed for ever and ever. Nan had been found in her hiding place under the parlour table, in spite of the plush table-cloth that nearly reached the floor. She had stormed and kicked and shouted and finally had hopefully compromised by announcing that she would only go as a queen. This she imagined would be quite beyond her mother's contriving, but her mother was a woman of spirit who felt a moral obligation to the organisers to send her children to the carnival. She snapped, "Right" at Nan, "You shall go as the Queen of the Flowers. I'll make a pink paper dress and sew it on your best petticoat. You shall have a crown of paper roses and a basket of flowers like a brides-maid. Lovely it'll be. You wait. Mammy'll make it real pretty." Nan went away to kick the front door, and heard her big brother say, "But w'at will you do for a mask?"

Around the table in the middle of the field the committee and the judges found themselves suddenly, quietly alone, like a shipwreck.

"Be on time for the demonstration tonight, remember. Ten-thirty prompt, mind." Old Eye began clucking again, important. "I better remind the boys w'en we say w'ose won."

"And tell them to bring some food and water with them if they can, it's hungry work walking . . ."

"Hullo, boys, look w'ose comin'," Eye interrupted D.J. as two uniformed figures came through the gates. Not carnival uniforms this time but serious uniforms. They held the two constables of Cilhendre. They walked like deacons into chapel, looking big in their buttons, but, close to, they were seen to be wearing their everyday, doing-a-bit-in-the-garden faces, not their point duty masks.

P.C. Thomas, the older of the two, asked in a cracked, pale voice if he could have a quiet word with D.J. The Magistrate felt sick in his heart whenever he had to do anything with the police. He hated prosecutions like persecutions and inside was afraid of the bobbies. He hated signing summonses, but stayed on the Bench because it gave him a chance to help some poor devils sometimes. He was honest, however, and knew about his weakness. He put on his talking-to-the-police face, his voice became slightly higher in tone and he pulled his self-confidence back by its tail.

"Well, Thomas —"

"Sorry to trouble you like this, sir, but we've got some bad news and we want your help, sir, please. It's the Manager, Davy, we've found him dead, mun, and with the Inspector in Brecon – to tell the truth, Davy, we haven't had much to do with bodies. Nobody's ever been found dead here like this in my time – except in the pit of course, but that's different and indeed, sir, I'm not sure what we ought to do about it."

The policeman's habitual blankness and his insensitivity had melted away like chocolate in the sun. He was frightened, nervous as a butterfly. His hands trembled. D.J. put out his own scarred hand to steady him, to remind him of his buttons, his majesty. The young policeman beside him, young Wilkins, looked pale green under the peak of his cap. He stood rigid, like frost. D.J. asked him if he was all right.

"Yes, sir. It was the flies, sir. All over his face."

The memory brought back a flush to the green face and D.J. remembered that he was only a young chap under those buttons.

"Will you come with us to see him, Davy? The Inspector can be so nasty to us chaps, but he won't say nothing to you, and if you'll excuse me, sir, nothing I do for the old Inspector is right. He calls me Duffer Thomas and makes fun of me, nasty."

"Of course, of course, come you. We'll go now together and you can tell me all you know on the way. Where is the poor fellow?"

"Down by the river, by the new bridge."

"Wait a minute then and I'll tell the others that I've got to leave them."

He turned to the table. "Look, boys, I've got to go some-where now with Thomas and Wilkins. I'll see you later. Don't ask any questions now. Let it lie a minute."

"All right, D.J., but try to come back."

The three walked away together, D.J. in the middle, look-ing small and arrested.

"How did you come to find Mr. Nixon, Thomas?"

"It was Mrs. Nixon, Davy, she came to the Station after dinner, see, and said her husband was missing. She said he'd gone out about eleven last night for a walk round. Said he often took a walk before going to bed – we said no more about that, Davy, but everybody knows where the Manager goes at that time of night, when poor old Elwyn Jeffries was working nights, whatever."

"No ill of the dead, Thomas."

"Well, sir, Mrs. Nixon said she hadn't been much surprised

when she found his bed had not been slept in – she said he was depressed about the strike and might have gone for a long walk to think things over. Awful thing, mind you, when a woman has to make excuses like that. But when dinner-time came – only she said luncheon – and no manager, she thought she'd better see us. She may have wanted to teach him a lesson. The boy was with her. Nice young chap he is too, great comfort to his mother that boy is. She said she was wondering if some of you boys on strike, beggin' your pardon, Davy, might have done him some harm.

"So Wilkins and me went to walk round and have a look and see a bit of the carnival too. We was watchin' for them to cross the bridge and I turned round to spit in the river and, diawl, mun, there he was. I swallowed my gob, couldn't spit on the Manager, whatever, and down we goes to have a look. He was dead right enough. Suicide, with having this old strike on his mind."

"Perhaps it was on his conscience, Glyndwr."

"No, I don't think he was troubled with one of those, Davy. But him and the Inspector are big buddies and I have to mind my words."

D.J. could not accept the policeman's theory of suicide. Not for the Manager – he hadn't the guts, nor the humility. The village was quiet now as they hurried to the river. The colour and shouts and songs of Carnival had swept over it, leaving a flotsam of papers and dust and a few women still hanging about their doors. The women watched the three men pass and then turned again to each other, their eyes speculating, like rooks. D.J. nodded to them and hurried on, his chest tight in the heat and the hurry and his heart sick with anxiety. What capital would the Owners and the papers make of the Manager's death? Was he going to be given a martyr's crown, this bully, this whoremonger, this boss? Perhaps boss was D.J.'s strongest word of condemnation, a word of real abuse from that gentle man. He wanted to believe Thomas' theory of suicide, but found he could not.

The River Tawe was almost sacred to D.J. It figured in most of his best poems; naively he had thought of her as the Maiden raped by the mine-owners. Now, when he saw the Manager fouling the river with his big, brown-suited, full, coarse body, he wanted to pull him out, to stamp on this beast, this enemy, but, as usual with D.J., wisdom prevailed and the poet gave way as he knelt on the river pebbles by the poor corpse. He saw the hated face, pale, mouth-opened, the eyes glazed, blood-bespattered and the bloated blue-bottle flies already laying clutches of neat white eggs along the edge of a cut like an open mouth on the back of the head. The man lay prone on the river stones, as though about to drink, but his head was turned sideways and the water rose only to his nose; all around him, hard and comfortless, were the river pebbles, uncovered now in the summer drought.

"Poor fellow, poor fellow," he spoke quietly. He had seen many dead bodies in his time in the pits, but down there, in the decency of the dark, they were more respectable and there were no flies, only the clean coal dirt.

"Will we move him, D.J.?"

"No, no, leave him. Get something to throw over him and leave Wilkins here to send all the spectators away. The Inspector will have to see him as he is. I'm not so sure about suicide, Glyndwr."

While the policeman went off to get hold of a blanket from the nearest house, D.J. was left alone with his old enemy. He had already seen that this was no suicide, that the Manager had not given himself that blow on the head. Thomas, as the Inspector had said, was a duffer and the flies had so sickened young Wilkins that he had not seen anything properly. It was no good trying to fake things, they would have a post mortem anyway. There wasn't anything he could do to help whoever had done this thing. But what was he thinking of? – he was a magistrate – this was no way to be thinking. Nevertheless, as he scrambled up the shallow bank to the road again, he scuffed his feet in the grass and the dust. He looked about him in the sunshine, too hot now and hesitant, not knowing what to think nor quite what his reactions were. He knew he was trembling, that his chest would not let him breathe, his thoughts came jumbled and unexpected. He was frightened and worried, appalled and even jubilant. The enemy, the symbol, was destroyed; but someone would be called to answer for it – someone he knew, almost certainly. Would it affect the strike – would there be waverers? Would the miners lose support if this could be pinned to one of them – or a gang of them? He had begged them not to be violent, to use their heads, but who could blame them? Thou shalt not kill. Yes, yes, I know, but thou shalt not oppress either, nor bully, nor threaten, nor covet and get thy neighbour's wife.

From this kind of frenzied thinking D.J. knew that only one thing would deliver him – talking to his mother, hearing her sanity. He'd put it all behind him until he got home.

The two policemen came back with a sateen quilt, hand stitched in geometric patterns, butter yellow on one side and blue on the other; a lovely thing, but even in death the manager was The Manager. When the body was decently covered D.J. told Thomas to telephone to the Inspector at Brecon, to tell the doctor and then to go to Mrs. Nixon to break the bad news. Young Wilkins, with his back turned to the quilted bundle, was left like a young knight to his vigil. The noises of the returning carnival echoed hollow under the cool bridge and kept Wilkins' mind off the flies.

CHAPTER 4

While P.C. Thomas telephoned to Brecon, D.J., weak and ill and trembling, drained by the shock, grey-faced, hurried away from the main road and, skirting the hill, clambered over his own garden fence to get home without seeing anyone. He was stumbling up the garden path when he was hailed by his next-door neighbour, Gerwin Evans, a tall bony man of about forty-five, a collier, with streaky grey hair, pepper and salt hair, that grew in a stiff coarse whirl around his head, all the hairs in the same direction so that there was no parting. His hair had once inspired some wag to call him Heavenly Land, but the name had failed. He was a serious, sad man, devoted to his widowed mother and to his sister, with whom he lived. His sister, Gwen, had the "decline" – and had not been out of the house for over a year.

D.J. knew that things were hard next-door. The two families were very close. The dull misery on Gerwin's face as he stood tearing bits of green out of the hedge recalled D.J. from the horror of the last hour. As Gerwin spoke, he pulled himself together, making himself think of his hands and feet and backbone and tightening the muscles. This was a trick he had invented and it helped him now to shake off his self-indulgent weakness.

Gerwin was talking about Gwen. "She's very bad there, Davy, the doctor says there's nothing he can do now. She doesn't seem to be trying no more. I am sorry to bother you, Davy, I can see you're in a hurry, but I had to talk to somebody, you don't mind, do you? It's been so quiet down here today with the carnival at the top end. I feel that something is coming over me. Davy. Christ, Davy, I'm afraid. I must have some company."

"Steady, boy, steady." D.J. tried to soothe him as he would a frightened horse underground. For the second time that afternoon he put out his scarred hand on another's arm to strengthen him, to be with him. "Come into the house to talk a bit, Gerwin. Mam will go over to your mother. The women are better there now, perhaps."

"Thank you, Davy, if you're sure you don't mind."

"Mind? No, no, come on, you."

They went together into the small grey house and D.J. was soothed and eased by his familiar surroundings. He was home again for a while, anchored to the dresser, the corner cupboard, the kitchen table with its red plush cloth and the settle by the fire with a red paisley cushion to match the stockings on the legs of the table.

Ann Williams was alarmed to see them and her stomach constricted when she saw the colour on Davy's face, looking as he did when there had been a bad accident underground, with those scars standing out like small blue worms, the one on the temple twitching on a nerve there. But she was not one given to excess in her behaviour and she waited quietly to hear what Davy would say. All he asked was that she should go next-door to Mrs. Evans while he and Gerwin had a chat. She nodded and without speaking threw a small triangular shawl over her shoulders. Under cover of these movements she indicated to Davy that he should get Gerwin to eat.

Gerwin stood at the window, looking out, seeing nothing. He tapped his long fingers on the glass, his big feet were on the bottoms of the lace curtains, pulling them out of the bow with which they had been tied back. D.J. left him there while he filled the kettle and put a white cloth on the table. There was a saucepan of broth simmering on the hob of the back kitchen fire; D.J. poured some of this into two basins with a design of red poppies on them. He cut slices of his mother's home-made bread and carried the food to the kitchen where Gerwin still stood and still beat his fingers on the glass.

"Come and keep me company, Gerwin, while I have this broth – we'll need something if we go on the march tonight. Come on, boy, there's plenty, look."

"I couldn't eat your food, Davy, it's too scarce to give away."

"Tommy rot, come on, Mam had this bit of lamb from her cousin in Myddfau, one of their own sheep it was. Your mother won't have much time to think about cooking with Gwen so low. Pitch in, boyo, it'll put some heart into you."

The "cawl" was excellent – with leeks and a suspicion of marigolds. Gerwin was obviously very hungry and ate ravenously, tearing the bread and sopping it in the broth. D.J. ate quietly without looking at his companion, then he began to talk about their plans for that night's march. The strikers in Cilhendre were to meet on the Square, the old village green, and there to wait for the miners from the Amman and Swansea valleys. Together they planned to march peaceably across a common, a sort of rift valley to the other side of the mountain, where one of the coal owners, still independent of the hated Combine, lived in his fine large house. They hoped to speak to him personally, to put their case to him so that he might speak for them to the other owners. They were simple men, not economists. D.J. was to be one of the deputation who was to speak, but his heart was no longer in the plan. He wondered whether they ought to go at all, now that the Manager was dead.

Gerwin had relapsed into silence again. D.J. tried to interest him by telling him of the Manager's death and his own fears of the results. But Gerwin didn't seem to hear, his eyes stared, big with their own anxiety and his hands had a bewildering, twitching, dancing life of their own, beyond his control.

D.J. got up and, lifting his mother's large, fat cat out of the armchair at the fireside, he led Gerwin to the chair. He made him sit and gave him tea, pouring it into the saucer so that he could hold it to his neighbour's mouth. The tea was warm and sweet and slowly brought some colour back to Gerwin's face and the life back to his eyes.

"I'm sorry, Davy, I don't know what's coming over me. It's the thought of death. Of not seeing her again for Eternity."

"Come, come, Gerwin bach, you must try to be more of a realist. You believe in Heaven and the Life Everlasting, don't you? We'll all meet again in the Hereafter, boy. Try to think like that now. Blessed are they that mourn, for they shall be comforted."

"Don't, Davy, don't say that. The Gates of Heaven are closed to me for ever."

"Stop this now," said D.J., his patience suddenly finished. "You're a good chap; you'll go to Heaven if any of us do; remember your Bible and come and wash these dishes with me in the back. We'll go over and see how things are with your mother after. She may want you to do something for her. Have you got coal and sticks in, and plenty of water? She won't want to go out to the tap in the dark. Mam will sit up with Gwen tonight while we go on the march. That will take your mind a bit."

Man-like the two carried out their dirty dishes, one thing at a time. Gerwin bringing in his miner's hands a flowered basin, empty now but for the starred rim of fat, holding it tightly with the concentration of a drunken man. D.J. washed the dishes in a blue enamel bowl and Gerwin dried them with great sweeps of the towel.

When all was done, Davy cut some more bread and a piece of Caerphilly cheese and packed them into his food box, the wedge-shaped, flat, strong tin box that all miners have to keep their food from the rats. He filled two pop bottles with water from the tap outside and put them into the pocket of his overcoat.

"I'll take my coat," he said, "and a muffler. It'll be cold coming home no doubt."

He was already desperately tired and dreading the long walk across the Common, shying away from the melodramatic picture they would make with their torches in the dark, fearing that perhaps there would be violence and foolishness. He had not slept well the previous night because he had been distressed after talking to some Irish miners who lived in lodgings in the next village. They had nothing to live on but their Strike pay and when their beds were paid for there was little left for food. They got one meal each day at the Soup Kitchen but very little else. People with families were better off because wives and children could claim Parish Relief, others had brothers or sisters at work, colliery officials, railway men, shop assistants. Nearly everyone could turn somewhere for help but these poor Irish were in a pitiful case and D.J. was upset about them, feeling responsible and guilty.

He had taken his walk and slept when he got back to bed but he had not slept enough and was now aching to take off his boots and close his eyes. Gerwin was on his hands, however, like a baby whose father is minding it while the wife goes shopping.

"Jawch, I'm a bit tired, Gerwin. I didn't sleep much last night. And I don't suppose you did either. Were you sitting up with her all night?"

Gerwin did not answer but looked at D.J. with such stark misery in his eyes that D.J. knew there was no hope for a little rest before they set off. Gerwin would have to be kept on the go. Pulling together all his very strength, from his toenails, he put on a heartiness and a briskness that would have deceived no one but Gerwin.

"Come on, then, let's go to your mother's."

They left the sanctuary of D.J.'s kitchen and walked through the gap in the hedge to the next house. It was the same sort of house, there was the same reverence for the old oak furniture, the same partiality to enlargement of the dead, the same pattern of living, in a kitchen which was the centre of the house, with a best room used chiefly for funerals and called "The Room" and a back-kitchen for washing and cooking. There were parrots on the wallpaper of "Cartref", parrots suspended on bits of trellis. Luckily many of them were hidden by the framed texts that hung on the walls and by the printed and framed sermons of several famous Welsh divines. There was an enlargement of Gerwin's father over the mantelpiece, taken when he was a young man with side whiskers. There was a dresser with Willow Pattern plates and Staffordshire figurines. One of these was turned with its face to the wall; it was a figure of Bonny Prince Charlie whose smug gallantry had made Gwen hate him. Her bed was in the kitchen, under the window.

She lay there with a stunned, flushed face, her eyes slightly popping and deeply shadowed. Her hands were bony and long with huge wrist bones showing below the cuff of her long-sleeved, frilled white nightdress. Her hands pulled and tortured the fringe of the white honeycomb counterpane which covered the bed. The room smelt heavy with sickness and chips and lavender-water.

She did not turn her head when the two came into the room.

"Hello, Gwen fach," D.J. said with a bluff heartiness that was as hollow as a coffin, "feeling any better today?"

She smiled thinly but made no other response. Death was so obviously near that Davy felt it was almost irreverent to speak to her. Gerwin left the kitchen again to pace up and down the garden path, the two women were busied with little important things. They talked in a forced, stage way about inessentials, their voices unconcerned but their eyes and gestures weighted beyond bearing.

D.J. sat quietly near Gwen's bed, relaxed beside her, glad to be there but feeling utterly inadequate. Men, he thought, were not much use at the beginnings and ends of life, but they saw to it that they dominated its little midday businesses.

Gwen turned towards him slowly and heavily and took his hand with a clumsy hot gesture; she began to sing in a harsh, cracked whisper a little Welsh folk poem:

> "Mae 'nghalon i cyn drymed a'r march sy'n dringo'r
> rhiw,
> Ac esgus bod yn llawen nis gallaf, er fy myw.
> Mae'r esgud fach yn gwasgu mewn man nas gwyddoch
> 'chi,
> A llawer gofid meddwl sy'n torri nghalon i."[1]

Davy tapped her hand and nodded while she sang on, missing and slurring many of the words. His heart felt twice as big and he turned his head to hide his eyes. Gwen was exhausted by her effort and sank into her pillow and into some strange depths where no one could follow. She took no more notice of the people in the room, her dark pop-eyes staring and glazed and horrifying.

The evening slowly tortured itself away. D.J. found it increasingly difficult to keep his thoughts on the now quiet girl, on death and heaven and fundamentals. Here was the threat and promise of death with him in the room and his mind must keep running off to temporary, transient things like speeches and committees and organisations and murders. Why did the big subjects always take second place, were they in truth boring? Perish the thought.

D.J. bestirred himself and offered to carry water in from the tap. His mother followed him outside.

---

1. My heart moves as heavy as the horse that climbs the hill
   And I can't for my dear life pretend to be happy.
   You know nothing of the place on which my shoe is pinching
   And many, many troubled thoughts are quite breaking my heart.

CHAPTER 5

After D. J. Williams left the Welfare Field and the procession came back, the carnival went on like a day by the sea. The news of the Manager's death had not yet whispered through the village. The holiday was still on. Sweating fathers killed themselves to get the kids to race, organised and tidy; kids went mad like dogs and the dogs thought their day was come. Mothers marvelled and boasted and cried a little and heard who was getting married and who had to. The Impossible football match went on and on, with no rules and no ref. and no end and far too many balls.

Important as a jury, Old Eye stood up at the judges' table and tried to be heard. Nobody listened. He shouted and rapped the table. He might as well have shaken a puny fist at the sun. He stamped his feet and got really furious; to save him from a stroke some of the Committee went over to the Red Indians. They told them to play "God save the King" on their gazooks. After the first few bars everyone was so surprised that they were quiet with shock. Eye took his chance. "Comrades," he shouted into the quiet, "Comrades bach, me and the committee have decided on our verdict."

"Guilty," roared the Indians.

"Now I am not going to make a speech —"

"Hoorah-ray-ray."

"Just a few lines as it leaves me at present —"

"No thank you, Eye, put a sock in it, boy."

"Wrap it up and take it home with you, love."

"My friends by here and me have decided to give the first prize to —"

"Me."

"Will you boys be quiet?"

"Yes, sir."

"Right. Now we have decided by here to give the first prize —"

"To our Maggie May."

"Damn you, will you be quiet for half a minute?"

"Who's using language? Shame. Shame."

"Oo, give him a chance too, fair play, hush now."

"First prize to Mairwen Morgan,

"Second prize to Ronald Evans,

"Third prize to Enid Davies and consolation prizes to Joe Davies' twelve." Eye reeled off the winners like a gramophone, breathless. His announcement was greeted with a thunder of shouts and groans and giggles. Before losing the limelight again he held up both hands, like a bishop.

"I have an important announcement to make. Don't forget, boys, the march tonight will start from the Square at half past ten. Bring some food with you, if you can; if you can't, bring some water to drink, whatever."

While the winners went up to the table to collect their prizes, the football teams sang again "Are we downhearted?" The girl who took the first prize, a half-pound bar of Cadbury's, was a fair, slim, pretty little piece dressed in a sack on to which were sewn empty pea-pods. On her back she wore a card which read "No more Peace", for in that valley she would pronounce peace and peas in the same way. Her buttocks wobbled free under the sack and she made the most of her legs. She ducked her head as she ran towards Eye and held her sack down with her arm along her thighs. There were appreciative whistles and requests for "points" and a share of the chocolate.

When all the prizes had been distributed Old Eye announced a "Scram" to console the children who had not won a prize. He walked away from his table of authority and stood, like Canute or God, with a large bag of "hard-boils" in his hand. The children surged around him, leaping and dancing, clapping and shouting. He dipped his hand into the bag and brought it out full of sweets. For a powerful moment he kept his arm poised then he threw the sweets at the children. They charged the falling sweets like tough little winds teasing fallen leaves, a storm of kids, snatching, grabbing, clawing.

God threw handful after handful at the children, pelting them, stoning them, lashing them. It was primitive, like Africa or the Roman Circus or sadistic dreams. He emptied the bag, put it to his mouth and blew it up. He clapped his hand to the balloon bag but the noise was too great to tell whether it banged or not. Throwing the bag at the children, he strolled back to the table again. As he walked, he wiped his hand down the leg of his trousers but he couldn't get the sticky off. He lifted his hand to look at it and saw that his fingers were all stuck together. When he opened his fingers little threads of elastic dirt ran from one to the other, grand-children's fingers. He walked to the table, but there was nothing else left to do. His official duties were over, the king was dead. Eye sat down and drummed his sticky fingers on the table and wondered again what was keeping D.J. and what the police had wanted.

Blodwen Bevan, the fairy who wet her knickers, was too late for the Scram, but she was to enjoy a greater treat. She became the centre of a Sensation. When her mother took her home they passed the house from which the policeman had borrowed the quilt to cover the Manager's body. It was the house of one of the firemen. Firemen were not on strike and this fireman's wife had not wanted to spoil her husband's chances of promotion by going to the carnival. The policeman had told her that the Manager was dead and that he was down by the river. She had been standing at her door ever since but no one had passed until Blodwen and her mother came, returning to the carnival. She was bursting with the news, aching to tell someone, anyone; she was the first to know, a keeper of treasure, confidante of the police. Mrs. Bevan came like a dose of salts for her. All that had been bottled up came out and Mrs. Bevan was suitably flabbergasted.

No fairy flew faster than Mrs. Bevan back to the field. She trotted off in that kind of jog that women over thirty-five call running, dragging Blodwen along. Her breath was in her fist, her eyes were wild and there were big arcs of sweat under the armpits of her best dress. Her big breasts thumped up and down, like galloping cart-horses. Blodwen's nose was running just as fast as Blodwen was but there was no time to stop and wipe it. Blodwen, in her tinsel, sniffed.

They got to the field and Blodwen and her mother had their hour. They told the news to the first group of people near the gates.

"W'at d'you think? The Manager's dead. Down by the river."

"Go on, you, no such luck."

"Yes he is, then," said Blodwen, cheeky now, with dry knickers and something to say. "Mrs. Rees Fireman told our Mam."

"You don't mean it, Maggie?"

"Yes, drop dead now. The polices found him, and Mrs. Rees lent her best quilt to put over him. Oh yes, he's dead all right."

"Awful, isn't it, girl?"

"Well, what killed him then?"

"They don't know for sure. Down by the river he is, drownded."

"For shame! Fancy! Hey, girl, what about Jess? Goin' to tell her?"

"No, not me, you tell her."

"Not for the world."

The stone had been dropped into the water and the ripples spread. You could see them in heads that came down to listen, in faces looking incredulous, in hands that covered whispering mouths, in shocked gestures, in serious faces that repudiated, in irresponsible ones that grinned and then thought better of it.

Jess Jeffries was standing with some of her neighbours in a gossiping huddle when the daughter of one of them ran up. It was Nan the Rose Queen. She pulled at her mother's skirt and whispered to her listening head. Her mother shook her and said, "Oh! There's lies."

"No, Mam, it's true, honest, you can ask anybody."

"What is she saying, Bessie?"

The child had their attention and rushed in with, "The Manager's drownded down by the river. Somebody pushed him in. It's true, cross the Bible, the polices found him."

"No. Never. Duw Mawr."

Jess turned grey-white and her upper lip began to twitch. She didn't say a word. She stood and tidied her white gloves, stretching them over her fingers and flexing them. She kept her head down. The atmosphere was thick, like a wedding. The other women pretended not to notice, but peeping, too, to see how she took it. After she had said the Lord's Prayer to herself three times, leaving out the bit in the middle about leading us into temptation, which she always forgot, she was able to lift her head and take herself in hand.

"Well, I don't know about you, but these shoes are killing me, standing about. I think I'll go home now. Elwyn can bring the children."

"All right, Jess, I'll come with you. I've had enough too, in this heat."

Together Jess and her next-door neighbour pushed through

the crowd. Heads turned to follow them and Jess's untimely departure put the official seal on the rumour.

As the story spread, it grew like dough in a warm pan. The Manager was dead in the river. Drowned, no doubt. Some of the strikers had done it. This was murder and Davy Williams had been seen with two policemen. Arrested probably.

Eye still sat at his table, wondering what else he could do to show that he was still top dog. The top dog who didn't know the secret, had not heard the news. A man stepped out from a group of people and walked towards Eye, walked with head down, too serious for the carnival. Eye wondered why.

"There's a rumour about, mun, that Mr. Nixon is dead. Have you heard anything?"

"W'at did you say? The Manager. Are you mad or w'at? The Manager couldn't be dead."

"Well, there's people saying it, whatever."

"Twt-y-baw, if the Manager was dead they'd 'ave told me. Wouldn't they? I am the Chairman of the Strike Committee. They couldn't have the Manager dead without tellin' me. Could they now?"

"Well, I don't know, indeed. It's Maggie fach told us by there and she heard it from Maggie Bevan. She went home to change Blodwen's knickers and Mrs. Rees Fireman told her then."

"Duw Mawr! I've heard my grandchildren sayin' some bit of a poetry about 'How do you know, Duck Luck? Hen Pen told me. How do you know Hen Pen? Chicken Little told me.' You don't sound much wiser, myn uffern i. *I'll* go and find out."

"How?"

"Well, I'll ask."

"Who will you ask? You can't go up to the house and say 'Please, Miss, is the Manager dead?'"

"Don't talk daft now," said Eye, like broken wind in a bottle, "I'll ask Davy Williams, he'll know."

"Somebody said he's with the police."

"Diawl, yes, he is too. Well, myn uffern i, there's a go. Hey, we can't have a carnival by here and him lying dead. We'll have to clear the field."

"Find out a bit more first. Come and ask a few with me." Suddenly the spirit of carnival ebbed. People still hung about in groups, uncomfortable and embarrassed. They trickled out of the field, were aware again of how foolish they looked in their silly clothes. They felt like Sunday mornings after Saturday nights. They were not sure how to behave, over-anxious to behave properly. Their clothes made things so much more difficult.

It was the Red Indian Band who started to sing, quietly, an anthem, a much-practised choral piece, the words from the hundred and third Psalm:

"The days of man are but as grass, for he flourisheth as a flower of the field. For as soon as the wind goeth over it, it is gone: and the place thereof shall know it no more."

Those who could joined in with the Indians, and thereafter the situation became orderly. The right thing had been done.

Only the children could not understand why the sun was no longer warm, why the tide had come in and driven them away from their day at the sea; why their parents hustled them home, why the day was finished.

CHAPTER 6

Inflated and restored by his new role as the bearer of important news P.C. Glyndwr Thomas rang the bell at the Manager's house. It was a grand house by Cilhendre standards. A large, old farmhouse adapted to its new station in life by the insertion of two imposing bay windows and a flush lavatory. There was a lawn at the front, crazy paving up to the front door and, on either side of the door, two white urns in which red geraniums grew. The door was painted black and the walls whitewashed.

P.C. Thomas rang the bell. A girl in black with a white cap and apron opened the door. Thomas knew her well, but allowed no sign of recognition to show.

"Can I see Mrs. Nixon, please?"

"Have you found him, Mr. Thomas?"

"Be quiet, girl, I want to see Mrs. Nixon."

"Well, you might give us the tip, mun."

"That's enough."

"Oh, all right. Spite."

The flowers and the heavy, shining furniture discomposed Thomas in some measure. He walked carefully across the hall, afraid to slip on the polish. He always had to remind himself that he was a member of The Force (Capitals) whenever he went anywhere that was grand.

Mrs. Nixon came to the door of the drawing-room from which she had watched his arrival. But she did not hurry, she waited dignified and restrained. She closed the door behind them.

She was a fairly tall, thin woman, with one of those cloche-hat middle-class faces. Faces that speak only with the lips, eyes that are silent. Repressed by good manners, she was like a grate decorated with a paper fan, never meant for a fire. It would be impossible to imagine her in bed; her tweed suit seemed as much a part of her body as her neat, uninspired hairstyle. No one would know that there was flesh and bone under her fine lisle stockings. To try and imagine anyone making love to her was like a crime against the Trinity.

"Good evening, Thomas, you have news for me?"

"Oh, hullo," said Thomas, flustered. "Yes, Mrs. Nixon. It's bad news I'm afraid. Try not to take it hard. We have found Mr. Nixon down by the river and he – er – he's passed away, like."

"What do you say? He's dead?"

"Yes, m'm, he's gone to a better world. Drownded."

"I see."

"Don't you take on, Mrs. Nixon fach. Sit you down by there. The Inspector said on the telephone, all the way from Brecon, that he was very sorry indeed and he'll come and see you as soon as he possibly can."

Mrs. Nixon did not sit down, however, nor, to Thomas' great surprise, did she show any of the symptoms of taking on. She stood, in the middle of the room, her hands held behind her back, feet set squarely, like a girl guide.

"Very well, Thomas, thank you. I shall wait to see what the Inspector has to say. Good-bye, and thank you for coming here. It was a hard task for you. Thank you too for organising the search."

She rang the bell and Rita, the girl who had answered the door to Thomas, came to show him out.

"Good-bye, then, Mrs. Nixon."

"Good day."

He left the room. Rita was still on pins to hear.

"What is it Mr. Thomas, mun? Tell a girl."

"Well, he's dead, that's what it is."

"No! Indeed to God?"

"Yes, and you had better go to that poor widow woman, by there. She'll be needing someone, no doubt."

"No, not I. I wouldn't dare. Not till she rings. So long. Thanks for telling."

The front door was closed and Thomas returned to the Police Station, bewildered by Mrs. Nixon's behaviour. No tears, not a sign of grief, no women's carry-on; he couldn't believe it. Her husband has been bad to her but he was dead, wasn't he? You didn't ought to take news like that as if it was the cat having kittens. They said she'd been to college, perhaps that was why. Great thing education, no doubt.

When Rita closed the door on Thomas she ran to the kitchen. The other maid was waiting to hear.

"Liz, he's kicked the bucket. Thomas Police came to say."

"You don't mean it? Honest? Well serve him right, the old ram. Come on, we'll have to draw the blinds, with him dead. Have you got a mourning hankie? Stop grinning, girl. We'll have to look upset, whatever. Pity for him, too; I'd hate to be dead, wouldn't you? Specially summertime."

"Wonder where he is by now. Will he haunt us, girl?"

"Don't be daft. He's safe enough. He's in the bottomless pit, that's where he is."

"Well, I hope he stays there."

"Come and do those blinds."

"Let's do them together. I'm afraid by myself. And for God's sake put the lights on first."

They ran from room to room in the quiet house, drawing down the heavy, brown Venetian blinds that rattled like dry bones. They knocked at the door of the upstairs study where John, the son, worked. Mrs. Nixon herself opened the door.

"Could we draw the blinds down in here, please, madam?"

"You have heard, then. No, please don't disturb us now. I'll ring when I want you."

"Yes, madam. We're both very sorry . . ."

"Thank you."

The girls scuttled off like two mice to sit in the kitchen and wonder.

Mrs. Nixon closed the door firmly again and went to sit on her son's bed. He was still at his table at the window. His head was down, his pen in his hand, he was filling in with it every loop in the letters of the page before him; carefully filling every hole up. He looked up at her and shyly took her hand. Tortured, clumsy, mumbling, he took her hand and held its dryness for a moment. His face was flushed as he stood and turned to the window. He tossed his head on his thin delicate neck, like a flower on a stalk. He breathed deeply, assumed a poetic otherworldliness. His shoulders were thin, his limbs stiff and ungraceful. Embarrassment choked him.

She understood; the girl guide said, "It's almost time to eat. I'll go and change into something black. You'd better wear a black tie."

"I haven't got one."

"I'll get one of your father's."

"No."

"Very well, we'll buy one tomorrow."

His mother went out and left him by the window. He watched the last children picking up bits of the carnival in the field, the discarded artificial flowers, the feathers, the lost ball. At last, only the rubbish that not even the children treasured was left to the grey sheep who now came back to claim their territory.

He turned away. His father had looked like a successful, seducing, self-confident fairground attendant. On John Nixon's slim neck the same face, refined and tortured, was like a Resurrection, a second coming, through fire. The likeness to his father went deeper than strong, thick hair, straight nose, well formed lips and teeth. It lay in his irritability too, which he attributed to his artistic temperament and, much more, it lay in his sensuality, in what, in his father, had been called "beastliness" but which might in him be poetry. He was his father's son, fretworked by his mother. He went to the bathroom and made a great business of washing. When he joined his mother in the drawing-room she was dressed for her part. She wore black marocain and a silver buckle on her belt. Her shoes were black, patent leather, long, narrow, with one bar across the instep, ladylike.

"I'm expecting that unpleasant Inspector Evans. Shall we eat quickly so that we need not ask him to join us?"

They crossed to the dining-room which was heavy with mahogany and gloss, velvet curtains and etchings. The meal was an unhappy compromise between Mrs. Nixon's upper-middle-class, moneyed background and her husband's studiously forgotten antecedents. It was a late high-tea which she called the evening meal, wishing she could say dinner.

She enjoyed the meal that evening. It was a conspiratorial, amicable, silent meal. They decided, calmly and rationally, not to discuss the situation any further until they had seen the Inspector. He arrived, with a noise like falling biscuit tins, just before eight. Rita, with a black and white hankie tucked into the waistband of her apron, showed him into the drawing-room. The Inspector came in red-faced, like an angry boil. A tall, broad man, with white hair and a white military moustache, full as a balloon of his own esteem; he had screwed the cork down on his bad temper as he rang the bell, but it was still there, ready to blow the cork.

"Good evening, Inspector."

"Good evening, Mrs. Nixon, and you too Mr. John," he said, shaking hands with each in turn, drama in every eyelash.

"Won't you sit down, Inspector. Whisky?"

"Thank you very much, as you're so kind. Well, Mrs. Nixon," profound breathing, "I cannot tell you how sorry I am about this terrible tragedy."

Mrs. Nixon nodded and waited. John poured whisky and water.

"To think that last night we were in this room together, playing bridge. Happy."

"Yes, but please tell us some of the facts. We know nothing but that my husband has been found dead, believed drowned."

"Well, now, I have been down to the river and we have brought his poor body to the Police Station. The doctor has seen him and says death was due to drowning; the doctor won't commit himself about the time of death. He's old and old-fashioned. Why, in Scotland Yard the doctors can give you the time of death to a fraction of an hour, so I'm informed. All that O'Grady will say is that he died after nine last night and before three o'clock this morning."

"How was he drowned? Did he fall into the river?"

"No, there's much more to it than that. There's a big cut on the back of his head and a bruise like a map on his chin."

Mrs. Nixon sat quite still and straight, knees together, feet together. John paced up and down the room, from the door to the window and back again. It got on the Inspector's nerves.

The Inspector sipped his whisky and went on. "There is a mystery here which I haven't quite fathomed yet. That fool, my P.C., decided it was suicide, but that is out of the question."

"What do you mean, Inspector?"

He took another long sip and a deep breath. "It wasn't suicide and it wasn't an accident. Something worse."

"Please stop this beating about this bush; if you mean murder, say so."

"All right, damn it, I will. Murder it is."

"Are you sure?"

"No doubt at all, none whatsoever."

"Why could it not have been an accident?"

"Can you tell me how a man could trip and fall on his face, getting a terrible blow on the chin, roll over and get a cut on the back of his head which would have felled an ox, and then roll over again into a convenient shallow pool? No it's out of the question. This is murder, my friends," Mrs. Nixon winced, "and I shall find the culprits. Oh, yes I'll find them, never fear. He was only drowned by minutes, the blows would have killed him, too. To say he was drowned is really only – what's that word now – academic, that's it. That's what the doctor said."

"But this is terrible. And at such a time."

"At any time. Why now in particular?"

"I was thinking of the strike situation. But go on please, tell us all you know."

"I was up in Brecon today and Thomas phoned me. He told me about the finding of the body and he said it was probably suicide. I came back to Cilhendre as fast as the Rover would take me. She's a lovely little driver and I think I averaged twenty-five coming down, with a short spell at the Bwlch because the engine was boiling over. I belted down to the Police Station to find Thomas. He said he had been to see you."

"Yes."

"Well, I bundled him into the car and he showed me the place. It's down by the new bridge. I parked the car where the old road joins the main road there —"

"Yes, but please get on."

"We scrambled down the bank, it's only a few feet to the river bed." The Inspector was not to be hurried. "There was a constable there with the – with Mr. Nixon. There he lay, poor fellow," all the stops out, "the sun was going down over the Drym and shining red on the river and he was there, under a quilt. It was all so wrong. It's a damn shame, that's what it is."

The Inspector put down his empty glass. John replenished it.

"There were no marks on the stones, of course, by then, nothing to show how he got there. There were plenty of marks on the grass on our side where my men and D. J. Williams had been mucking about, tramping all over the clues. I went up to him and when I had the quilt off I saw the wound on his head and the bruise, I decided at once it was Foul Play. It's those damn strikers, mark my words. I don't know what the country is coming to. Suicide, indeed. No. Somebody helped him out of this world, Mrs. Nixon, and I am going to find out who it was."

"Will you?"

"Of course."

"What have you discovered?"

"Well, I've got a clue. Wait till I tell you. While we were looking about I happened to notice that somebody had been digging on the far bank; it was fresh digging and untidy, though the sun had caked the top soil. I wondered what it was all about. I was desperate for a clue, you see, and I had to try everything. We borrowed a spade to see if anything was buried there and, my God, there was! Mrs. Nixon." He inched to the edge of his chair. "It was a grave – the grave of a newly born baby in a coffin. It was a small coffin, lined with white silk and a little ugly baby inside. Jawch! you could have knocked me over. The doctor said there was no foul play, that the baby was still-born. But of course the law has been broken – all births and deaths must be registered. This isn't China yet, thank God, where you can throw your babies away if you don't want them, just like that," with a

loud snap of his fingers that made Mrs. Nixon's flesh creep.
She wondered about poetic justice, and the Inspector continued, "Mind, I don't know if the two things are connected.
What I thought was that your husband might have seen
somebody burying the baby and he was killed for what he
saw. Or, at least, whoever buried that baby may have seen
something to help us. It's a clue anyway. Now all I've got
to do is to find out who was preg – in a certain condition
and we will get somewhere. I am sure nobody could be
expecting in this village without everyone knowing. The
old women seem to know before the girls themselves."

Mrs. Nixon coughed at the Inspector and glanced at John.
Putting his foot in even further, he said, "Oh, beg pardon,
I'm sure." John pretended he had not heard.

"I don't envy you your task, Inspector. I expect you'll find
the village people will stick together over this. There won't
be volunteers with information, there is too much bitterness
against my husband. The people will not care about the
abstract notion of seeing justice done. They may feel that
justice has been done. Would it not be better to save face and
ask for an open verdict? Found drowned. It would save
every one a lot of trouble and embarrassment."

"Mrs. Nixon, I'm surprised at you. I can't understand you
at all."

"Can't you?"

"No. Damn me, I can't. Is it flesh and blood you are,
woman, with your husband brutally murdered, to sit there,
as calm as a pancake, running him down and teaching me
my own job?"

"It might perhaps be better if I acquaint you with some
facts, not, mark you, suppositions. Not the kind of whispered
gossip that has been circulating in this village about my
husband, but an authentic account from an eye-witness of
where my husband went last night. You were here, you will

remember, until about ten o'clock or thereabouts. After your departure I retired, as did my son, leaving my husband alone in this room. It was our habit to leave the room at night before he did, for I had no desire to watch him contriving excuses for leaving the house.

"As I say, we went upstairs. John sat writing for some time and, hearing his father quietly leaving the house, my son, in a sudden, perfectly natural impulse, decided to join him. John thought they might walk together and perhaps come to a better understanding of each other, he thought that his father might in fact be lonely. My son has a right to his own opinions of course. However, John, having taken off his clothes, had to spend a little time dressing himself again and his father had gone some distance ahead. It was too late to call after him, at that hour, so my son hurried after his father whom he saw disappearing around the corner to Gough Street. Gough Street leads of course to the canal bank as well as to those dreary streets called after the South African Campaign and John assumed that his father would walk beside the canal, which, since it is disused has become a pleasant enough place." Mrs. Nixon went on in her cold expressionless voice, feet together, hands, still, in her lap, head well up. "Before John could make his presence known to his father, my husband paused at a back garden gate, watched a light shine on and off several times at a window and then, furtively, loathsomely, bestially, he crept down through the garden and in at the door of the house." There were two spots of colour in her cheeks and a slight tremor in her voice, due entirely to disgust.

"Now, I'm sure John would not have betrayed his father to me – for it was in the nature of a betrayal – were it not for my anxiety this morning when there was no trace of my husband. He felt that I should be in possession of as many facts as possible. Do you now want to bring these facts out to the light of day? Would you have my son testify against his father's name? Will you allow my affairs to be turned over in public by every Tom, Dick and Harry, like – like women turning over second-hand clothing in a market-place? Is that the measure of your friendship for him? And think of the woman, you would ruin her in a place like this – perhaps she deserves it, but the real fault was his – there is her family too. Take what the gods offer. Say he was 'found drowned'. You cannot afford to antagonise the village people now, Inspector. These are difficult times and some of the good people are almost desperate."

"Good people, did you say? Damn strikers. We ought to shoot a few of them to show who's boss around here . . ." Taken aback and blustering. But he couldn't bluster away her persistence.

"I don't like the story of the baby's grave. They will feel it was a desecration to dig it up. Where is the baby now?"

"Up at the Station, of course, until the inquest on it."

"I trust you are treating it properly, Inspector. Someone must have felt very deeply about that child to have buried it with such care and tenderness. That little coffin; it's all so horribly sad."

"You seem to care more about that baby's body than your own husband's. If they thought so much about it, they should have reported it honestly, and had it properly buried with everything in order, not this fly by night way and breaking the law."

"See to it please that the body is treated with proper reverence."

The Inspector sat on in his chair, trying to get his attitudes straight again. His part in the play had been the bluff and hearty friend of the deceased who would comfort and support the widowed, meanwhile sorting out the tangled clues which would lead the criminal to the scaffold. He had picked up the wrong clue at some point and found he was in the wrong play after all.

John came and poured a third whisky into his glass to give himself something to do with his hands. He never smoked at home.

"Thank you. Now then, Mr. John, perhaps you would like to tell me a little more about this walk you say you took."

"I followed my father out. He went through our back gate, past the Church and tennis court and along the fence of the Miners' Welfare Field. Then he followed the Canal Bank to the backs of those houses that have their gardens along it. He turned in at one of the garden gates and when an upstairs light had been put on and off a few times in quick succession, he went in at the back door."

"Which house was it?"

"I don't think I am going to tell you that."

"Damn. Is this the co-operation you're giving me?"

John was silent and blushing down to his neck.

"Excuse me now, sir, good night."

He walked out of the room, tossing his hair from his eyes. He closed his eyes as he fumbled for the door-knob and tried to push away the memory of how last night he had envied his father his easy conquests.

"Do you know who the woman is, Mrs. Nixon?"

"Yes. But I don't propose to tell you, I'm afraid."

"Oh, indeed, obstructing justice now is it? Well, if that's the way it is, I'd better go."

The Inspector got up, and for the first time in his life left some whisky in the bottom of his glass. He was moved. "I've got a busy night before me, with this terrible thing on top of the miners' demonstration tonight. I am sorry you feel like this. I was counting on your help and sympathy with my work, but, there it is I suppose. Yes, I am disappointed and shocked to the core." He thumped his core and this made him cough and choke on the whisky. "We'll take formal evidence of identity tomorrow. I shall have to ask for your presence, but I will telephone you in the morning."

Rita came to show him out. She thought his parting with Mrs. Nixon was a bit short. He didn't answer Rita's "Good night, sir." He growled and muttered to himself and stamped to his car.

Rita was sorry for the poor Rover.

CHAPTER 7

It was nearly quite dark as the strikers gathered that night on the Square. They came slowly and doubtfully, not sure now that it was right to have their demonstration. They came with their friends, their butties, and stood about in the patch of open ground that was used for auctions and small fairs on the Square. Acetylene lamps had been fixed to posts and these hissed and flared and lit up men's faces. Gold faces and black clothes; deep caverns of noses and pits of eyes; water bottles catching high-lights. John Nixon, who was watching them, on his own, as usual, and very aware that he was alone, thought the scene was like an Old Master, painted in a wild enthusiasm for chiaroscuro. The Night Watch, he thought, or the Syndics of Cloth Hall. Women and children stood near the edge of the waste ground, like doodlings on the side of a page, cut off; leaving this to the men.

From about ten o'clock the men began to assemble. D.J. came with Gerwin, Jack Look-Out with Tommy Davies, Everynight, Cow-and-Gate, Jim Jesus (he did not believe in voting, because the Lord will provide, but he was on strike, fair play). Jess's husband was there with Ronald, the second prize winner. The Square slowly filled. There were shouts and ribald comments, with snatches of singing, but the spirit had gone flat like stale beer.

D.J. was very doubtful of the outcome of the march. He had had a bellyful of violence for that day and was wondering why they had ever thought of this crazy idea. They would not do any good.

The wildest rumours had percolated through the village at first, but the news about the baby had defeated speculation.

The story had spread like syrup, but the simple, sentimental people had failed to come to terms with it. No one was known to have been as pregnant as all that. Perhaps it wasn't anyone from Cilhendre at all.

Before the arrival of the strikers from the other valleys the Police Inspector drove up to the Square in his Rover car. The two police constables were with him; Thomas at his side and Wilkins perched high in the dickey, matching the Rover mascot on the bonnet. The car stopped. The Inspector tooted imperiously for silence and then stood on the running board, facing the colliers.

"Men," he foghorned, "I have two things to say to you. First, I warn you, there must be no breaking of the peace tonight. We want no more trouble in Cilhendre. But if we do have trouble, we know what to do about it. The other thing I want to mention is the unfortunate death of Mr. Nixon, your colliery manager. I want anyone who saw Mr. Nixon at any time after ten-thirty last night to come to the Police Station in the morning. Anyone of you who thinks he has any information which may help to solve the mystery of the Manager's death, must please come to tell the authorities as soon as possible tomorrow morning. One last word: it will do you no good to break the peace. I give you fair warning."

He climbed back into his car, turned it with a flourish that failed, because he was not very sure of the gears, and set off in reverse. Neglecting his clutch and making a racket like his own swearing, he finally made the turn back to his Police Station, with Wilkins hanging on to both sides of the dickey, his knees by his nose, his helmet down to his knees.

Into the silence after the Inspector's car had jarred away on the edge of their teeth, there came to the crowd the sound of tramping feet in the distance. A cheer went up and the strikers formed themselves into a straggling untidy column;

committee at the front, friends together, a bit like silly school girls. The posts carrying the acetylene flares were pulled up and carried high in the crocodile, D. J. Williams was up in the front thinking "I hear the tramp of armed men." He was cold in his belly, tired to death and so worried that he was no longer sure what he was worried about. His thoughts played peep-bo with his mind.

When the leaders of the other column came in sight, excited and friendly, D.J. asked a committee member to run to them with the news about Mr. Nixon and the Inspector's warning. The news went whizzing down the column but, as they had come so far, the men would not consider turning back now. They set off quietly and sedately, they might have been going to chapel. Word was passed down that they would go first to the Manager's house, to sing a hymn, to show their sympathy and that there were no hard feelings. "The days of man." They straggled along, heavy-footed in working boots, and packed the road outside the house. There they stopped, took off their caps.

Hearing the noise, Mrs. Nixon looked out of her bedroom window, frightened for a moment. She looked down on a dark congregation, she saw the caps come off, the lights shining on bald heads, grey heads, one bright golden head and then the tenors started to sing. Music was lady-like when she was young and it was permissible to be moved by it. For once in her life she was at one with the colliers. Music, that knows neither class nor country, the most civilised, most sophisticated achievement of men, thawed her cold face, softened the lines. Her nostrils quivered.

"The days of man are as grass, for he flourisheth as a flower of the field. For as soon as the wind goeth over it, it is gone; and the place thereof shall know it no more."

When the anthem was finished she hurried to her front door, and as the procession formed again she lifted her hand slightly from her side and whispered "God bless you." The miners thought she was nice to come out. Her son, who had walked alongside the men to his own home, waited until they had all passed on. He recognised few of them, so changed were they by the dark and the flaring shadows, men of the choirs, of strikes and pubs and chapels and kindnesses.

They passed him into the shadows, a black river of some of them hungry, many of them tired, all of them loyal, bitter, driven too far. His father had been of the enemy, but they sang for his mother and nodded capped heads at him. No hard feelings.

He crossed the road when the last man was gone, when the tramp of feet was a whisper. He went into the dark house and shivered. The August night was chill now, after the warm day, but his mother allowed no fires until October. The kitchen would be warm.

He walked down the grey stone flagged corridor to the kitchen door. He heard the voices of the girls and, remembering Rita, her shape, her vitality, the willingness in her eyes, he turned back again. He muttered, "Lead us not into temptation," and went upstairs to take a cold bath. This had always been recommended at his school as a cure of flesh.

He called, "Good night" to his mother and went to his room.

CHAPTER 8

The Miners had gone into the night. Hundreds of men, an army, like the Pied Piper's rats. Cloth-capped, heavy footed, mufflered, dark-suited, ungainly men, underground men, flowing like an underground river suddenly broken out. They talked and teased and grumbled and sang as they walked, these ragged soldiers, these tidy men. They sang anything that had a good tune for walking and a bit of easy sentimentality to it, The Red Flag, Calon Lân, Land of my Fathers, Lily of Laguna, All by yourself in the moonlight. One end of the column might be pushing their feet with hymns while the tail might swagger along to Music Hall.

Women with children stood at lighted door-ways to see them pass. Some of the children were frightened by so many men in the dark. They hid their faces or turned to stare back at lighted kitchens and known fireplaces.

The men went on – men going begging.

They passed the last houses in Cilhendre, passed the Railway Station, trucks on the siding empty and hollow. The flaring lights trapped the white painted names and passed on – Powel Duffrin, Crynant Colliery, Amalgamated Anthracite, Brynhenllys, Seven Sisters. In the lights, the grease in the boxes on the trucks burned golden and oozing, the labels there washed blank by the sun.

After the Railway Bridge were no more houses. The road began to climb and twist, hung with heavy August trees. There was no singing on the hard hill, breaths were preserved to help the tired feet. The coughers walked slowly and stopped and lost their places.

The top of the climb brought them out on to a strip of

common and moonlight, a rift that joined two valleys. Here the road ran between high banks grassed over. On either side were open spaces of rough, reed-like grass crossed by a few thin brooks. There were leeches in pools in these brooks and watercress and a ghost haunted the left-hand bank of the road.

They waited a spell when they reached the Common. Perhaps they stopped because no one wanted to be first past that ghost, an old man with money, from one of the farms, who could not pull his earth-bound spirit away. There were some who said they had seen him. Just short of the ghost they decided to rest before walking down to the next village which was where the Mine Owner lived.

The column split. They sat down, stiff, leaning against the banks of the road or squatting on their haunches. Some spread out on to the grassy common. They relaxed, ate their food, swigged from the water bottles. A few had beer on tick, just for tonight. They ate and talked and passed the bottles.

Jack Look-Out sat with his neighbour, Tommy Davies. Tommy should never have tried to go on the March. He was not on strike and was physically quite unfit for the long walk. He had come with the boys, however; staying at home he would have felt dead and buried already. The climb had nearly done for him, but Jack's arm was strong and they had come to the Common at last with the other stragglers. Late, they were isolated from their Cilhendre friends and sat together alone. Their nearest neighbours were two deacons, talking sermons. In the privacy of the sermons, Tommy was able to say what had been on his mind since he heard of the Manager's death.

"Jack, boy, are you going to tell the 'spector that you saw him, Nixon, last night?"

"And put my head in a bloody noose? No."

"I don't know, mun, if you went and told the truth honest

and said where you seen him and when, they'd think it wasn't you did it because you volunteered."

"No bloody fear. Everybody knows that time when I'd had a couple of beers I wanted to tar and feather him. I said in front of Glyndwr Thomas Police that I'd swing happy for the bugger. If they knew I'd been talking to him last night it would be nappo for me, boy. Look out. Honest volunteer myn uffern i, double bluff they'd call it, sure as Sunday."

"You – you didn't do it, did you, boy?"

"No. But good luck to him that did, say I."

"What if somebody saw you out and tells?"

"Who the 'ell can have seen me? There wasn't nobody in the street."

"I don' know. Somebody else must have been about. Somebody did for him. And there may have been others."

"Here, have this last drop of beer and change the subject."

"Where did you have this drop Jack?"

"Maggie's."

"Pay for it?"

"Aye. Never you mind how."

"Oh that way, is it? Well, good luck, and if it's an alibi you want, boyo, I'll be there."

Jack gave him a gentle cuff on the ear and pulled his cap down over his eyes for him.

"Come on, come and look for the boys. I've had enough of these bloody deacons."

They worked their way through the groups of men, asking for Everynight, for Cow-and-Gate or Elwyn. They found them talking about the ghost and ghosts. Cow-and-Gate was saying, "I've told the missus enough about going to the Spirits. She goes down to that chapel they have in Clydach and comes home with diarrhoea and messages. For me mostly, to keep off the beer. From my old man too. Must be jealous up there, aye. She even had a prescription from a medium once. All fancy writing it was too, like the doctor. To put in my tea it was, to stop me smokin'. I gave her prescription! Mean lot they must be in Heaven."

"Oi, did you hear about old Joe Genteel's widow?"

"Don't tell me she's a medium, whatever. She'd finish off any spirits double quick."

"No, mun, she says Joe comes back to her. Comes back the minute she's in bed and starts."

"Drop dead."

"No, Jawch, old Joe had stopped years before they put him in his coffin."

"Well, he's had his second wind now, whatever. P'raps there's Spanish Fly up there."

"Duw! Fancy, with a ghost."

"Shut up now boys, will you, indeed. You make me quite upset. I been married twice, don't forget. If my first took a notion – I've hardly got the wind for one."

Cow-and-Gate was on the point of wondering whether the Manager would come back and if so to whom when he remembered that Elwyn Jeffries was there and heavily changed the subject.

"I wonder if your fox is out tonight, Joe."

"'Spect so. Let him enjoy himself tonight. I'll get him tomorrow and then come Saturday we'll go to Maggie's with the five bob and, boy, I'll order ten pints for us. Ten foamin' pints in a row on the bar and we'll drink 'em, boys, slow, relishin'. Will you come with us tomorrow night Elwyn? – Since you was with us last night, like."

"Aye, of course, I'll come. You bet."

Nothing was actually said, but Elwyn's alibi was established in case it was necessary.

Gerwin had followed D.J. all night. Always close to him, under his feet. Even when D.J. wanted a bit of privacy to be comfortable for the rest of the walk, Gerwin came too.

Davy wanted desperately to be alone, to give his mind to all his troubles. He wanted to think over what he should say to Griffiths the Owner, to get all his arguments and answers rehearsed. Whenever he let his thoughts hang loose he found that he was saying, over and over, "I hear the tramp of armed men, take George's pile and gravel pills." He could not remember for sure where the poetry came from, Scott, perhaps, but he knew that George's pile and gravel was in big yellow letters on Ystrad Station. Round and round it went in his head and he was too tired to stop it, like a child feeling sick on the little horses in the fair.

Davy shared his bread and cheese with Gerwin. They drank elderberry wine from the medicine bottle that his mother had slipped into Davy's pocket just before starting. The wine was thick and sweet and warming. D.J. passed the bottle to the strike committee. "Don't take too much, now, that wine is five years old, a drop will put a bit of life in your legs, but you'll go to sleep on a glassful, mind."

"Shall we go on again then? We don't want to be too late."

"Aye, let's go."

They groped stiffly to their legs; groans and coughs, rheumatic twinges.

"You shout, Maesgwyn, you got a big voice."

"Oi, we better make a start, boys, Cilhendre Committee is leading. Get fell in there. She had a good home and she left, right."

The beer and the rest had put more heart into them and Davy faced the ghost warmed by the elderberry.

As they came past the ghost's beat, where the trees grew near and it was very dark, two big, glaring eyes suddenly appeared. Before they could think, they were scared for a moment, but they soon recognised a familiar figure in the glare of a car's head-lamps. The Inspector's Rover was blocking the road and on either side of it was a dim fence of figures – about twenty, about forty or a thousand, in the dark.

The Inspector came to meet the strikers.

"Halt," he shouted. "Go back now, peaceably. We can't let you go any further. Mr. Griffiths has asked for police protection and, by damn, we will give it to him. Turn round now and be off with you."

Davy turned to the committee. "Come on, boys, do as he says. We don't want trouble. Let us go back." The nearest colliers heard him and there were shouts of "No. no." The end of the column wanted to know what was up. "Polices. It's the bobbies, won't let us go on."

The policemen had been drafted in from the neighbouring valleys and were there to hold the miners back, to teach them a lesson – or so the Inspector intended. The police were themselves as frightened as women. They had been waiting on the qui vive for hours, their nerves at a stretch. Some of them were frightened of the ghost, all of them terrified of the Inspector. He did not believe in ghosts. There were only twenty-five of them and there were hundreds of colliers. Some of them were colliers' friends but all were some Inspector's creatures. They did not like it. Their bellies felt like jelly.

"Are you going back?" Inspector Evans bawled again. The Cilhendre Committee turned and tried, with no hearts, to urge the others to go back, to shout yes, but someone in the back threw a beer bottle; it slid green past the headlights of the car. That was all the Inspector needed. He ordered the P.C.s to charge the men with their truncheons and they, poor frightened things, did as they were told. Glad to get moving. After the first head it came easily.

They swung their truncheons, fought, met little resistance, and succeeded in scattering the colliers. The colliers were afraid of policemen and especially of truncheons which were outside their experience. They turned and hurried back, appalled. The constables followed, carried away by a new-found sense of power. They began to enjoy themselves. When they had lost their first wind they turned back victorious, one by one, and felt terrible.

Those whom they had knocked out, they revived and bundled into the two old boneshaker buses which had carried the constables to the place. The buses were driven off, complaining, to Neath; to the cells. A few policemen were left on the Common to keep guard. The Inspector stood on his own dung-heap, cock of the walk.

In her spick-and-span, mind the cushions, don't sit on the three-piece, little grey house, Jess Jeffries sat in front of the kitchen fire; she sat with her knees apart, her skirt folded back to warm the tops of her legs. She stared into the flames and pushed the coals about with a thin poker. She had changed out of her navy blue best and wore her middling clothes, a maroon artificial silk dress with a flowered pinnie. On her feet were white sand-shoes. Her stockings were fawn lisle, rolled around garters above her knee. Big brown sausages of stockings, then large white thighs, slightly mottled, like alabaster, with blue, then apple-green, fleecy-lined knickers. You would need to be sitting in the fire to see all this, for she sat legs apart, monopolising the grate.

She wasn't enjoying her warm. When she was not poking at the fire she pleated up the bottom of her pinnie, making a fan and then pulling it out. Time after time, each pleat meticulously measured against the other and then – whip! – out. She scratched her head and dragged a heavy hand down from her hair, along her cheek, pulling her eyelid down, then her cheek and then her lower lip. She held her hand by her lip, little finger just caught by the overhang. She started to bite the nail, then brought the finger over to the other side, where she had more teeth. Then she passed her big hand all over her face, two or three times, squashing her nose and muzzing her eyebrows. Her nose was red afterwards and her eyebrows stuck out anyhow.

She picked up the poker again and made furious jabs at the fire. She threw it down on the other fire-irons – not for use, only for cleaning, brass, *H.M.S. Victory*. Jess stood up and looked for something to do. Sitting was no good. She couldn't make tart, the oven was cold. She had tidied the drawers, she didn't have anyone away, so she couldn't write a letter, the mending was finished and *Red Letter* didn't come till Friday.

Since she came home from the carnival, Jess had been finding herself things to do. Concentrating on the children, bathing them and washing their hair, combing the hair with a fine comb in case they'd caught anything at the old carnival. She cleaned all the windows and polished the brass, but now idleness had caught up with her. She had run away from herself until now, but the thoughts had won the race in the end.

Desperate, she put on the kettle to make a cup of tea; taking her time to fetch a clean cloth and one of her best cups with rosebuds. She went to the front door while the kettle boiled, but there was nobody in the darkening street. She came back alone. She sat at the table and poured the tea. Her left hand tapping, tapping on the cloth as she held the cup to her mouth. The light caught the thick gold band of her wedding ring. It was one of the few real wedding rings left in Cilhendre. You could always tell a cheap substitute because it left a grey-green mark no matter how much Brasso you used on it. Jess nibbled a Welsh cake with her tea.

When her cup was empty, she turned it upside down in the saucer to drain, then, taking the cup in her right hand, she swung her arm round three times towards her heart. She reached for the *Oracle Dream Book* and read her fortune from the cup. She would never see the want of bread, was what those crumbs meant. Those two bits like a bird at the top meant news. Thank you, she'd had enough news to last her. That thin trail of fine "tips" meant a journey. Pwff! there were no answers there. What about the cards? She shuffled and shuffled the slick, blue-patterned pack and drew out nine cards over the nine of hearts, the wish card. Nothing came right. There wasn't a picture among them and telling fortunes was hard without pictures. Five of spades was bad but nine of diamonds was all right too. Better cut again. No, she was no good on her own. She'd go and see Catherine Fortunes, that one was good. When she was going to tell you something really spicy, her neck would swell and her hands would shake. Oh, yes, she was clever, gifted, they said.

Jess took a second cup of tea and decided to go to bed. She built up the fire to keep it in for Elwyn and set out a clean cup and saucer for him, put a plate of biscuits on the table. She turned out the light and went upstairs. Flakes of whitewash fell off the ceiling as she walked heavily above.

It was a bed-ridden room; no room to swing a sock. Here she was quite alone, not even the fire for company. She had to face it now. She sat on the bed, twisting her wedding ring round and round on her finger. She undressed and in her big white calico nightdress, cut like a sack, her hair hanging in a plait down her back, she went on her knees to say her prayers. She said her prayers every night, even when the shining lino was freezing. But that night she prayed hard. Not only "Gentle Jesus, meek and mile" and "Our Father chart in Heaven"; she made up one of her own special prayers which she only did when things were really bad.

"Oh dear Jesus bach, keep it dark, will you love? Don't let it come out. It might be in the paper. Oh, Christ, for God's sake, keep it quiet. They would cut me out of the chapel, see, and whatever would my mather say and the old neighbours? No, you wouldn't let it come out, would you? I didn't mean no harm, honest I didn't. We've always been tidy people, God, and nothing's come out before. Oh, Jesus, ask your Father to keep it quiet. I'll never do it no more. I didn't mean it bad, honest. Amen."

She lumped into bed and pulled the blankets over her head to keep out the thoughts. She had great faith in the Lord and felt much better after her prayers, a step at least had been taken in the right direction.

She had had a long and busy day and soon she was asleep. She did not hear her husband come in during the night and he was undressed to his shirt when he woke her, shaking her shoulder and calling, "Jess, Jess."

She started out of a dream of – to hear him saying, "Wake up now we've got to have a talk."

Her heart went cold and bigger and she stayed down under the clothes, not looking at him. He sat on the edge of their bed in his shirt, his legs bare, hanging over like a boy's. He followed the check of the blanket with his finger. His thin, narrow, tenor's face was grey in the hard light that shone on the little bald patch that showed through his bouncy hair.

"Look, Jess, I know about him. I've known for weeks now. Even watched you givin' him signals with the light when I was out. I was mad. But then I thought it out quiet. I am on strike and I can't give the kids what they need. I didn't ask you or them if I could go on strike. I expected you to put up with it. But you and them aren't colliers. You don't understand. I haven't got no right to blame you for what you done." He got up and walked up and down the strip of room at the side of the bed. He swung round suddenly on the brass knob at the foot of the bed and said, "But, you bitch, couldn't you have found some other man, any other man, not that swine?"

"There wasn't nobody else and you needn't use language."

Jess started to cry quietly, wiping her eyes on the corner of the sheet.

"Look, Jess. Now don't cry. We've got to talk serious. You'll start remembering every funeral you ever saw if you start a good cry and we won't get nowhere. The 'Spector was on the Square tonight and he said for anybody who saw the Manager last night to go to the Police Station to say. Was he here last night?"

Jess cried quietly and turned to the wall.

"Answer, will you? I won't shout, honest."

The whispered "Yes" filled the small room.

"Are you going to tell the 'Spector?"

"Duw Mawr! No."

"All right then, don't say nothing. If they find out he was here last night and me out, I'll be the first they'll arrest.

They'll say I was jealous and I killed him."

"Oh, no. Elwyn, no."

"Of course they will, girl. Look a bit further than your nose for once, will you?"

"Oh, come here, love, and don't say such things. Come in by me, warm. They wouldn't dare and you so good."

He slipped into her arms and rested his head on her shoulder. He felt he was slipping into warm water and the sun shone warm for a spell.

"El," she said, in a while, "did you?"

"Did I what ?"

"Kill him."

"Damn you, Jess. I'll put up with your whorin' when we're hungry, but, by Christ, I'll belt you if you don't mind your words."

"Sorry, love, I only asked."

"Well, don't ask, then, if you can't talk civil."

She turned a lock of his hair round and round her finger, enjoying crisp of it. "Where was you last night, then, El?"

"Don't believe me now, do you? Don't kid yourself, my girl, I didn't kill your fancy man, I wouldn't risk hanging for him. Go to sleep now. I'm tired after all that walking."

"Was it any good?"

"No, the bloody polices sent us home again. A few in the front got hit."

"Well! Drop dead. Nasty were they?"

"Aye."

CHAPTER 9

There were proper cells at the Police Station at Neath. But they were few and it was not possible to give the strikers the very best accommodation. It would only be for one night and the authorities were not unduly worried. The thirty-seven men brought in from Cilhendre were first taken to the office. Here they gave their names: Canddylan Price (Eye), David John Williams, Gerwin Evans, Ceiriog Lewis, John Jones, John Lewis Jones, Evan Thomas, John Thomas Jones, Thomas Griffiths, the Jones' and the Thomas' came in a flood, confusing the sergeant. He was a good boy, that sergeant. He organised cups of tea for the men, sorry for the lumps and the bruises and feeling responsible. Away from the Inspector, the policemen won back their manhood and their humanity. The sergeant took Eye on one side and begged him not to worry, for the old man's defeated incredulous expression was daunting. "They'll only keep you in for tonight. Just a warning it is. Don't worry, Mr. Price, it's not as if you was in jail; look you're having a cup of tea. Come on, you shall go home in the morning."

When the tea was finished, the men were herded into the cells, five or six to each cell, with chairs provided for those who had no room on the benches. They were very quiet in their indignity. Bewildered and bemused by the injustice and the pains in their heads. D.J. was the only one of them who had even seen a cell before. For the others it was another world beyond the pale; chaps like them and the chaps they knew didn't go to jail. It was as far from their world as Buckingham Palace or P. G. Wodehouse. The policemen at Neath did not know D.J. He didn't tell them he was a magistrate. For them he was just a tired, defeated collier.

They passed an uncomfortable night in the cells. They tried to sleep sitting on the hard bench and the chairs. Those on the benches slipped over each other like dominoes, but it was worse trying to sleep on yellow, hard, slippery police station chairs. Like sleeping in a concert. Tired miners sagged in the chairs, big hands trailing to the cold floor, heads dropped slack like balloons after the party; mouths open in the grey faces where new beards sprouted.

Gerwin had stayed close to D.J. They were in the same cell. Davy was lucky to find a place on the bench but Gerwin did not sit. He stood, tall and gaunt, wide-eyed, looking round this narrow space with fear in his face.

"Sit down and try to sleep, Gerwin, boy."

"I can't."

"Sit down, whatever, or you'll disturb the others."

"All right."

They shuffled and fidgeted, rubbing their backs on the wall, trying to ease into comfort, turned on their hips, moved their feet in their working boots, avoided each other, apologised, slept stiff and unrelaxed, jerked awake and aware and slipped back again. D.J. resolutely closed his eyes and folded his hands. He must sleep. He would be ill without some rest. He tried to imagine how the nothingness was before God said "Let there be light!" and in nothingness he slept. Discomfort wakened him often and each time he saw that Gerwin was awake, staring. He refused to let pity seduce him and fell asleep again.

When the early August dawn was breaking, Gerwin put his hand out to D.J.'s knee and shook him. The nothingness before light was passed away, and the cells and the troubles came back.

"Davy, Davy, speak to me for a minute. I was afraid. You all look so dead, sleeping. It's light now, look, you don't mind me waking you in the morning, do you?"

Davy rubbed his hand over his face and sat straight. He tried to ease his bones, started to cough. He spat into his red handkerchief and, setting his hands on his knees, his head down, he stared at the floor of the cell. He murmured a quiet prayer that things would go easier today and asked for strength for himself and for Gerwin and for a bit of peace and quiet. "Davy, I wonder how she is by now."

"Yes indeed, boy, perhaps she's a little bit better again. Let's hope, whatever."

"Davy, while these others are sleeping let us have a little shat." (There are parts of South Wales where Welsh speakers find it almost impossible to pronounce *ch* hard as in chocolate. They would say ships and shops for chips and chops. Complications can and do arise, e.g. chit is a problem. Chain has by an extension of the process become shine, so that a lavatory has a shine.)

"You know the Roman Catholics, don't you, Davy?"

"Yes."

"Well, I was talking to those Irish boys once about religion and that, and they was saying that they can confess their wickedness to the preacher and then they can forget their sins. Is that right, Davy?"

"Well, it's like this, see. Their preacher isn't like ours. They call him the priest and when they speak they call him Father. They don't feel he is an ordinary man like themselves, but somebody very special, holy I suppose. The priests can't get married for one thing. They mustn't love anybody more than anybody else. A bit like Jesus saying 'Woman, what have I to do with thee?' to his mother. The priest doesn't have his own family, all the parish is his family and he is a father and friend to them all. Do you understand?"

"Yes, go on. Go on about the confessing part."

"Well, now, Catholics feel that the priest is nearer to God than they are themselves, and because they trust him, with

what is on their consciences, they think of that in itself as
an Act of Faith. They tell him all that they have done wrong
or thought wrong, and don't think that's an easy job now.
The telling by itself is part of your punishment. Fancy going
up to Morgans Bethel and telling him how mean and small
you really were. I couldn't do it, I know. But then, their priest
is different, see; in their eyes, whatever."

"Yes, and when you have told?"

"Oh, it depends. It's not just a matter of paying out money
for forgiveness and then finish, and roll on next pay day to
pay for some more wickedness. Oh, no, no, that's just a bit
of bad history we've been taught. I think that paying theory
comes from a long time ago, back in the Middle Ages when
Pardoners could sell you a pardon and a free ticket to
Heaven. But that's just a bit of bad in the apple. It's not the
truth of the matter. No, there's much more to it than that.
First you have shown this man all the evil in your heart, you
have made yourself small in his eyes – it's like 'unless ye
become as little children.' Then, I suppose, the priest tells you
that you have been bad and wicked but that the Lord's mercy
is infinite, like the sea. The priest decides what punishment
he'll give you. – No, he decides what penance you shall
make – there's a difference there I hadn't thought of before –
if it's a small thing you would likely have to say over a
number of prayers. I don't think much of making prayers a
punishment, mind. That's not my idea of prayers. The phrase
the Catholics like is An Act of Faith. They mean doing a thing
which proves you believe in the power of Christ to save and
God's will to forgive. You tell your sins, you ask forgiveness,
and in this way you show your faith. I'm not sure what sort
of thing the priest tells you to do if it's a bad crime you've
committed. But whatever you tell him, it's a secret. He
mustn't tell anybody at all, ever, not the police or anybody.
There was a king once I remember who walked barefoot in

the snow to Rome to get forgiveness. Hard work being a priest."

"It must be a great thing, Davy, to tell. It wouldn't only be a punishment. It would be like lifting a ton off your chest. Like the time I was trapped underground. I think telling would be like when they got the roof off my legs."

They talked in whispers, heads close; one on the bench, Gerwin on the edge of the yellow chair.

"What are the worst kind of sins, Davy? Sins of the flesh?"

"No, I don't think so, Gerwin. I think that not respecting other people, bullying other people, being blind to the feelings of other people, being self-righteous and unkind are the real sins. I don't think Jesus took much notice of the sins of the flesh. Mary Magdalene was his friend. And it was God gave us the flesh, Gerwin, after all. But, boy, what are we two old bachelors talking like this for? Not much comfort for the flesh in this old cell, whatever. My flesh could do with a nice cup of tea and no mistake."

"Finished the sermon, D.J.?" A collier in the corner of the cell stretched and yawned. "Aye, a cup of tea would go down lovely. What a night. Oh, well, it'll be something to tell the boys. Heroes we'll be, no doubt. Wish I had a big bandage on my head, like a picture we got in the parlour. Some poor devil of a hero from the South African War it is with a lovely big white bandage and blood. We don't look much like heroes in by here, do we? Look at us; there's heroes."

Slowly the two other men woke, disbelief in their eyes before remembering. They were stiff as beanstalks, yawning, small-eyed. The air was heavy in the cell and the bucket in the corner was unpleasant.

"Don't start thinking that you're a martyr, Sid. The police were quite justified in what they did. Whoever threw that bottle was the culprit. He broke the peace, the silly young devil. I said enough about doing what was right. We must be careful because we can lose sympathy as easy as breaking wind."

"They can keep their bloody sympathy," Jim Jones Full-pelt growled. "What we want is the Revolution. Duw! I've got my plans, mun, for when the great day comes. There's a few I've got my eye on. Stationmaster, for one, and Morgans Bethel. I'll deal with them personal. I'll strip those two and march them through Cilhendre naked and me with a sharp spike behind, proddin'. I'll show everybody they got belly-buttons and then that's them finished. You can't boss no more when everybody's seen you got a bellybutton same as they have. There's no power in a man when 'is belly's been on show."

Sid was meditating this theory. "Aye," he said, "that's one I'd like to see undressed, is Mrs. Manager. Now that one hasn't got one, I'm sure. Under her skirt, I bet, she's like one of those model women in Morgans draper's window."

"What'll happen to her now, Davy? She won't stay in the Company house for sure. Pity, too. She won't find it easy to be poor. She isn't used, like us."

"Don't go wasting your sympathy on her," the Revolutionary spoke again. "She won't be poor. She's got a tidy bit in her stocking."

"How d'you know?"

"Well, look at her face. Good God!"

"Yes, I think she's got her own money," D.J. interrupted. "Nobody could keep two girls to work, and live as they do, on Manager's money."

"I could do anything on Manager's money. Think of the feel of fifteen quid or more. Just think of the feel of it. Dei! If it was only for a week, boy. King of Cilhendre. Be as good as the Revolution, mun."

"You and your Revolution. That's not what we want. Look how the Russians have treated the churches for one thing. That was bad."

"I wouldn't care if they burned down Bethel, as long as Morgans was in it."

"Now, now, that isn't talking nice at all. Morgans does his best, fair play."

"Aye, his best. Frock coat, myn uffern i. But the vicar, now, I'll take my cap off to old Edwards. He's a real gent, even if he is Church. Have you ever been to Church, Davy?"

"Yes, I've been, but I didn't get the proper spirit, somehow. Silly, I know, but there it is. Mind, I love the Church when it's empty. There's more Grace in an empty church than in an empty chapel. Chapels are too light and yellow to have that kind of quiet. It's a pity we can't build better chapels."

"But Bethel's got the biggest pipe organ in the valley, mun. Iesu, I wish they'd bring some tea, whatever."

At eight o'clock, slow as time, the policeman brought tea and bread and butter to the cells. Sweet, strong tea, rust colour. And at nine o'clock, sharp as peppermint, the Inspector drove up to the Police Station at Cilhendre. He strode in, dancing.

"Good morning. Good morning. There'll be a nice few headaches in Neath this morning. We taught those strikers a lesson they won't forget in a hurry. Well, Thomas, what's wrong with you today? You look like a wet holiday. Take your finger out and look sharp. When the people come with information about Mr. Nixon I want you to take down their names and addresses and then send them in to me in my room. One at a time, mind. I don't want a crowd."

"Yes, sir. There's a bit of bad news this morning, sir."

"What?"

"Young Gwen Evans, Gerwin Evans' sister passed away in the night."

"Oh, too bad, too bad." Brisk. "But it was expected, wasn't it? Didn't she have T.B.?"

"Yes, sir, but Gerwin wasn't there and there'll be a lot of talk."

"What are you trying to say? Out with it, man."

"Well, sir, Gerwin is in Neath, in the cells."

"Humph, pity, but there, serve him right. He should have stayed at home at such a time, not carrying on like a hooligan about the roads. Can't be helped. It's too late to phone Neath now."

"Yes, sir."

"Now, remember, one at a time I said. But give me time to telephone Mrs. Nixon first. Found out who was pregnant yet?"

"No, sir."

Thomas sat at his table on the Police Station chair and copied out in Best Writing a list of names. They were the names of those in the cells at Neath. The names had been given over the telephone and Thomas was busy making a fair copy of his first hurried list. He was still nervous of the telephone and prayed his list was right. His left arm held the paper down like a convict, and his pen was imprisoned in a grip of iron, down close to the nib. He had blotting paper under his hand to blot each name as it was finished. His tongue was out playing follow my leader with his pen.

He wondered who would be the first to come to the Station. Time ticked quietly away on the Station clock, but just as Thomas was finishing his list and beginning to risk breathing freely, Inspector Evans volcanoed out of his room.

"Nobody here? Do you think they mean to come?"

"Perhaps nobody saw him, sir. Everybody goes to bed early in Cilhendre, not like London."

"Nonsense. It's a conspiracy, that's what it is, nobody wants to help the police. This damn village. It's the military we want here."

"Well, I didn't see him, whatever. I was on duty till eleven – and I waited about until 11.15 too and I didn't see a soul out – except Jack Morris Look-Out coming from round the backs and going up to his street, Mafeking Terrace. And then, when I was drawing the curtains going to bed I saw Joe Everynight and a gang going out for foxes."

"Oh, you saw something then did you? Weren't asleep all the time? Jack Look-Out, did you say? Isn't that the one who wanted to tar and feather my friend?"

"Aye, I did hear something like that."

"Well, that's one thing to start on. We'll see what Mr. Jack has to say for himself. I can see we'll have to go out ourselves, if we are to find anything out."

"Perhaps everybody doesn't know you want information. Everybody wasn't on the Square last night. You better send the clochydd round."

"Yes. You are bright this morning, for once. Must be the weather. Go and tell Wilkins to fetch Leyshon the Cryer while I plan out our campaign. We'll have to see D. J. Williams first. He may have noticed something yesterday and I'll have to fix the inquest with him and the doctor. And get him to sign the summonses."

"You can't do that this morning, sir."

"Why on earth? He's idle, isn't he? He'll be about."

"No, not him. He's down in Neath too."

"Christ, you don't tell me he's in jail?"

"Yes, sir."

"Oh, my God! What a police force! What can a man do with such fools? Taken the magistrate to jail; why didn't they look who they were hitting, for God's sake?"

"It was dark, sir. None of them is cats."

"That's enough. I'll have no impertinence from you, Thomas. Go and fetch that Cryer."

"Yes, sir. Here's the names from Neath."

The paper was snatched from Thomas' hand and the door of the Inspector's room crashed behind him. Thomas smoothed his hair, licking his wounds; and put on his helmet.

In 1926 there was still a village Cryer in Cilhendre. An old oldman who rode a donkey called Millicent. He lived alone in a dirty, window-broken, dirty white-washed, disreputable, henrunned, pig-smelling old cottage outside the village – alone with his donkey, his hens and his pigs. His clothes were ragged and filthy, his skin around his neck and under his hair flaked and caked with dirt.

Young Wilkins picked his way like a girl in high heels up to the door of the cottage. Chickens flew and a fine yellow cock advanced with his wings to the ground. Chicken houses bolstered up the cottage and the smell of pigs was like fog. Wilkins knocked at the door and called but got no answer. He minced through droppings to the back door and saw the old man in the garden, picking blackcurrants.

"Hullo there, Leyshon."

"Oh, w'at you want?"

"Inspector wants you. He's got a job for you."

"I got a job by here, thank you, pickin' currants."

"Lovely ones they are too, but you can do that after. Will you come to the Station with me now?"

"Oh, all right, again. I'll come, I'll come. Have to wash and change first. Come and see Thomas and Susan."

"Who are they Leyshon?"

"Here they are, my boy. The two best pigs in Cilhendre. Lovely. Twenty score Thomas is. Lovely pigs. Lovely pigs. Talk to them till I come back. They like a chat."

But Wilkins went to the currant bushes while the old man was indoors. He picked a currant but it tasted of pig. Leyshon called him in a while and said he was ready.

Millicent and Leyshon were dressed for the occasion. Millicent was wearing a sack on her back and a remembrance poppy in her bridle. Leyshon had on a long clerical grey mackintosh coat over his working clothes and a green bowler hat on his head. There was currant juice on his chin. The coat was his badge of office and in his hand he carried his bell. He mounted Millicent and set off with Wilkins at a funeral pace.

They went together into the sunshine and the sun was hot on their backs. The sun brought out all the richness of Mr. Leyshon's smells. They talked pigs as they walked. Leyshon was incensed because Tynewydd's boar had broken out one night and paid a visit to Susan. Now that Susan had clicked Tynewydd had the cheek to ask Leyshon to pay. Damn, they ought to pay Susan; they paid women in Cardiff so he'd heard.

Wilkins was glad to get to the Square. "I'll have to leave you here, Leyshon. I'm on duty, see?"

"All right, I'll go to the Station, go to the Station."

"So long then."

"So long, you."

When the Inspector's nose told him, before Thomas, that Leyshon had come, he hurried from his office with a piece of paper.

"Good morning, Leyshon."

"Same to you and many of them, many of them."

"I want you to cry this message, please. Can you read it?"

"I can't read that crow's feet writing. You read it out, read it out. Then I'll manage."

"Right. To the people of Cilhendre. Will any person who saw Mr. David Nixon, Manager of Cilhendre Colliery at any time after 10.30 p.m. on the night of August 2nd, please come to Cilhendre Police Station with their information. Signed, Ernest Evans, Inspector of Police."

"Read it agen, read it agen."

After three more readings Leyshon said, "Yes, I can read it now. Give me the paper. You haven't said any trimmings. I'll put them in myself." Suddenly Leyshon swung his bell in the Inspector's face and filled the office with hellish clangour.

"Gwrandewch i gyd. Gwrandewch i gyd. To the people of Cilhendre, village, in the parish of Dysul, Wales. Will any person who saw Mr. David Nixon, Manager of Cilhendre Colliery, owner, Mr. Griffiths, Blaennant, at any time after 10.30 post meridian on the night of August 2nd in this year of grace, 1926, please and thank you, come to Cilhendre Police Station, Cilhendre, with their information. Signed, Ernest Evans, Inspector of Police, God Save the King. God Save the King."

His voice hit the walls and ceiling and bounced back again. It set the bell on Thomas' desk quivering and the ginger mouse-cat crept flat under the desk. Dogs heard it in the street and dropped their bones. The Inspector set his teeth, and stood his ground: he had been in the Somme offensive. Thomas had his head out of the window, very interested in something outside; he had not been further than Brecon Barracks.

"Right. Right. I'll go now. Cry through the village and ten shillings to pay, please and thank you. God Save the King."

Leyshon collected his fee and departed. He left his echoes and his smells. Thomas opened the window top and bottom and put on the kettle for a cup of tea. The cat came back. When the tea was ready Thomas took a cup to the Inspector's sanctuary.

"Thanks. I've been making out our plan of action. We'll go over it when you've had your tea. I wish that man Leyshon would take a bath. He stinks like foxes."

"Yes, sir."

"Well, go along, go along, take your tea and don't be all day about it."

"No, sir."

As Thomas drank his tea his gulpings were accompanied by the far away voice of the cryer earning his ten shillings in the streets of Cilhendre. Thomas wondered if the money

was a good investment. His tea finished, he went out to the
little building behind the Station to look again at the baby's
body. Like a nosy old woman, he tried to give a name to
the face, but the little, puckered poultry-shop face told him
nothing. He touched the small doll-like hands and the cold
death in them was like an electric shock. He put the lid
quickly back on the coffin, guilty. The Manager's body was
lying there too, under a white sheet. He didn't lift the sheet
but left in a hurry, a frightened old woman. He locked the
door and hurried back to his office. The Inspector was waiting
for him. He let it be thought that nature had called him round
the back.

"Now, then, Thomas, this is what we'll do. You will fetch
Wilkins to take over here and then we'll do this interviewing.
We'll call on the doctor first to see if he's thought any more
about that baby. He may have remembered by now, old
though he is. Then we'll go to the midwife. You should have
thought of her before Thomas. I thought that Williams the
Roadman might have seen something when he was sweeping
yesterday morning."

"Yes, indeed. You got a good idea by there."

"Then there's that farm, Brynhir, it overlooks the river by
the bridge. It's possible they saw something from their
windows in the moonlight."

"Will we call at the farm?"

"Yes, of course."

"Bit of a job that'll be I'm sure."

"Why, man, it's not far to walk . You're getting fat, Thomas,
the walk up will do you good."

"It's not the walk I was thinking of, but never mind."

"Then for Jack Morris Look-Out, unless he's in jail."

"No."

"Well he ought to be. Now, Thomas, there's something I
want to ask you. It's about Mr. Nixon. Don't be afraid to

answer because he was a friend of mine, but I've been hearing some very funny rumours since yesterday. Have you heard that he was, well, friendly with a woman in the village."

"Oh, yes, sir, everybody knew that. He had a fancy woman right enough."

"Are you sure?"

"Well, I never saw them, not to say see, but I've heard plenty."

"Who was it Thomas?"

"Jess," said Thomas, feeling like Judas.

"Jess who?"

"Jess Jeffries, up in Mafeking Terrace."

"Big, dark woman? Didn't we have her husband up before the Bench for poaching salmon?"

"Yes, sir, let off with a caution. First offence."

"So that's who it was. I never dreamed of such a thing. Well, well, we live and learn."

"Do you think he was there that night, sir?"

"How should I know? But he was found between his place and hers, for what that's worth. All this is hearsay, though, and what have I told you a hundred times about hearsay?"

"Not evidence, sir."

"Right. But if he was there, where was her precious husband? His goings on will bear looking into. We'll have to see them both. We've got a busy day, my lad. Go and get Wilkins in!"

Thomas put on his helmet again and went out into the sun. He could still hear the Cryer in the distance. He was not feeling very happy about Jess, sorry that he had to be the one to tell; they used to be in the same class at school and she used to let him copy. He gave the message to Wilkins and they came back to the Station together. The Inspector was at the door, bursting to be off.

"Come on. Come on. Don't take all day. Get in the car

Thomas and you take over the office Wilkins. Anyone who comes with information take down names and addresses and a brief statement. I'll call on them later."

Thomas stepped high into the car and swung the curved door home. Wilkins thought the car looked like a high blue boat on wheels. It was the first car in Cilhendre. The Inspector loved it like money. The car jerked forward, stalled, reversed and suddenly was off like a bomb. They roared through the village, Thomas muttering prayers for deliverance and the Inspector enjoying himself, playing tunes on the rubber ball of the horn, deafening ears only just recovering from the Cryer's assault.

They drove to the doctor's house. The doctor was on his front lawn taking out a tooth with large silver pincers. His victim was a young fair boy whose father held him by the shoulders from behind while the doctor pulled like a fiend in front. The doctor won the tug-o-war with the help of a kick from the boy. Dr. O'Grady fell over backwards, waving the pincers, holding the tooth. The boy stopped yelling and started to cry quietly while the doctor got up and gave him the tooth and a shilling.

"Whist now, whist. Sure it's all right ye'll be in the mornin', all right in the mornin'."

"Thank you, doctor, thank you. Come you, Gwilym, it's all over now, look. Spit it out, boy, never mind the old blood. You'll sleep quiet tonight. Daddy'll give you something nice as soon as there's work. Come you."

Dr. O'Grady rumpled the lad's hair. "Sure isn't that the brave boy? Good day to ye both!"

"Thank you Doctor. Good day!"

He shoved the pincers into his poacher's pocket and came up to the policemen. He looked like a kindly brown bear. His tweed suit was shaggy and peat brown, and he wore knickerbockers which gave him that slimness about the legs which bears have.

"Is it yourself, Inspector? Isn't that a grand day?"

How the Irish doctor had first come to Cilhendre had long been forgotten, but he had married a Welsh girl and settled there more years ago than anyone really remembered He was a great Irish patriot and bitter as medicine about the Six Counties of the North. It was said his money came from Ireland. It must have come from somewhere for doctor's fees in Cilhendre would not feed a cat. He was always willing to take payment in kind, pounds of butter or a chicken now and then and he never refused a piece of old furniture or a bit of a jug that might have been on the dresser for donkey's years. The Soup Kitchen Committee had cause to be very grateful to him.

"I'm sorry to trouble you, doctor, but I came to ask if you had found out any more about that baby."

"Now what baby would yous be meanin'? Sure, there are so many babies."

"The baby we found buried by the river."

"Och, sure, the wee thing. Thon baby never breathed in this world, the poor wee enfant. There's no foul play and yous might save a poor girl's good name."

"Is this your respect for the Law, sir? Would you be aiding and abetting murder? I want to find out whether the people concerned with this are in any way connected with the Manager's death!"

"Devil a bit. Devil a bit."

"You don't know the mother do you, doctor?"

"No, I havena' been professionally consulted in the matter of thon. And sure, it's an old man I am to be keekin' the girls' shapes. Yous might try askin' the midwife, but. Belike she'd be knowin'."

"Thank you. The inquest is provisionally arranged for Friday morning. Does that suit you?"

"Yes, sure, that's fine, so it is."

The Inspector had a nasty suspicion that the doctor knew more than he confessed to. He climbed back into his car, malignant, and drove off to the midwife's house.

Old Cis had two important jobs to do in Cilhendre. She laid out the dead and delivered the babies. She was a little old woman, bent and wrinkled like a very old shoe. She wore black clothes and a man's cloth cap. When it was a birth that called her, she wore a black and white checked cap, for bodies she wore black. Under the peak of her cap, her eyes were snapping and sharp and dark, she had lost all her teeth and her long nose overhung her pursed, lip-less mouth. She could have passed for a witch, but was in truth a kindly, gentle old woman. She had living with her a family of children of different ages and appearance. They were all illegitimate children whose mothers had been unable to keep them. Old Cis brought them up and loved them and was good to them. She was paid a few shillings for the maintenance of each child and kept them clean and healthy until they were old enough to earn.

When the policemen called, Cis was just taking off her black cap which she had worn for the laying out of Gwen Evans. She was in a hurry to be off again.

"Good morning, Mrs. Owen, could we have a word with you, please?"

"Well, it'll have to be a short word. I'm in a hurry. If you look up the mountain you'll see a big white cloth out on Bryngolau field; that means she wants me and she always wants me in a hurry. Gets them easy as spitting but I want to be in time today. This is her seventh and she's a seventh. Seventh of the seventh brings luck."

"All we wanted to ask was whether you knew who was the mother of the baby that we found buried."

"No, I don't, and if I did it wouldn't have happened. I know the regulations, reading and writing or not, and I always like things done right. No, I can't help you, sorry. Can't think who, to tell the truth, and it isn't much hides from these old eyes. Got me beat this time. But I got to run, honest. Go now, indeed. I'll come and tell you if I hear anything. So long now. Must put on my other cap, white apron. Here's my bag. So long."

His morning's interviewing discouraged the Inspector; he was hungry too. "Thomas, we'll leave things here for now. Go home for your dinner hour and meet me again at the station. Don't be late, and don't eat too much, we've got to climb the mountain."

"Right, sir." Thomas was suspiciously cheerful. The Inspector wondered why.

CHAPTER 10

The Strikers were allowed to go home after their breakfasts. They were not charged. They had been detained for their own good, to help them keep the peace. They set off to walk home together. They went quietly through the town before the shops and market were properly awake. The town was quiet like a church. The shops were full of impossible riches and the dummy ladies beckoned to them through the windows. A bed in a furniture shop was pink and seductive. D.J. wondered who bought such things; were there so many whores? They passed the railway station, that smelt of fish, and crossed the bridge over the River Nedd. Sea birds swept up and over them and then stood like an army of spectators along the bridge. Rotten carcasses of boats mildewed in the river and on the left stood a tall grey factory where nobody worked. The gulls made derisive noises at the colliers, telling the world they'd been to jail. The town straggled on in villas until it was another village; slowly the pattern of the valleys was asserted; village after village climbing higher into the hills, deeper into the coal, further into the depression. The surrounding hills crept closer and warmer. The people no longer stood apart from the colliers with the superior, studied indifference of the townsfolk. The colliers no longer felt clumsy and foolish, Taffy from the valley; their steps began to ring confident and home was near and perhaps praise.

They came to the Common where last night had been last night and met there a great and wondrous quiet, the tumult of grasshoppers and the curlews and the thin water-cress brooks. They stopped to rest there as they had done before. Some took off their boots and paddled their feet, Gerwin

84

Evans went up one of the streams and, lying on the bank, he caught three small speckled trout that were hiding under the big stones. He wrapped them up in fern leaves and carried them in his cap. Gwen might like them.

Left to himself, D.J. slipped into his sheltered poetry world. He sat staring at the fat black-brown leeches in a pond and tried to get on with the lyric that was on the end of his tongue, like a forgotten name. He was trying to resolve for himself his own problem of poetry – how to write what was true to his day and his suffering without cynical pretensions and yet true to the glories, the everlasting benison, without sentimental shudders. It seemed the Welsh tongue was not designed for this. For fine-wrought, over-wrought poetic gymnastics, yes, for biting, bitter, cynicism, yes, for thick, spongy sentimental gush, most certainly, and for hymns and sermons, but not much good for the uncertainties and hesitations that were the truth. Words and phrases clicked in his mind but his critical faculties were sharpened by the open common, the joy of a warm morning with a splendid sun, and no words were good enough.

The arrested strikers arrived in Cilhendre while the women were cleaning and the policemen interviewing. They went quietly to their homes; it was mid-morning and broad daylight, not a time for demonstrations. As Gerwin and D.J. approached their houses they could not fail to see that the blinds were drawn in the windows along the street.

"Davy ... those blinds are not for Manager. Do you think —"

"Come on, let's get home. It's no good wondering."

In "Cartref", Gerwin's home, the truth was only too apparent. Gwen's bed was no longer under the kitchen window. The room had the newly tidied look of a hospital ward before the doctor comes; there was an impossible neatness, and Mrs. Evans looked dusted and rubbed and set in her place on a chair by the fireside. Her clothes were black and her face yellow and old, old. Ann, D.J.'s mother, was with her and Bonnie Prince Charlie was again smirking into the room. Gerwin stood at the door, blinking out of the strong sunlight.

"She's gone, then?" he said.

His mother nodded and jerked out her arms towards him. Gerwin stumbled to her and bumped to his knees at her feet. She held his big body close and looked over his shoulder, wordless, remote, her tears falling unregarded over the yellow, lined skin. The man did not cry but in a minute lifted his bewildered head. He faced the dresser over her shoulder. He wrenched away from her and stretched his long arm to the Bonnie Prince. He dashed it to the floor, smashed it on the flags, but the head snapped off and rolled away with the gay, dashing, stupid smile intact. Gerwin was after it and stamped on the face again and again. When it was finished he slumped into a kitchen chair by the table and hid his face in his arms, as though suddenly ashamed of the unseemly display. D.J. tried to think of something to say, something to do, with his hands and feet. He put his hand to Gerwin's shoulder and pressed it.

"Fear no more the heat o' the sun," he murmured inadequately, criticising himself for having said "o" for "of" so pedantically. His mother swept away the bits of the Bonnie Prince and, with no further word, mother and son left the house and the mourners to the privacy of their grief.

"So you've been in jail, Davy?"

"Yes, Mam, are you going to cut me out?"

"Did they hurt you, my boy?"

"No, it's all right now. But I'm very tired. I think I'll go and lie down for a bit. There'll be a lot to do later on. They'll want me to write letters next-door, and I'll go to Evans Funerals for them. But I must have a rest first, Mam. I'm fagged out."

"Yes, you go to bed and I'll make some dinner. I wonder what would draw Gerwin to eat."

"Make a few chips, they're always appetising."

"No, indeed, boy, chips in a house of mourning, that would he sacrilegious!"

Fortified by their meals, Inspector Evans and P.C. Thomas faced the long walk up the mountainside to Brynhir Farm. The farm overlooked the river and the bridge, where the manager's body had been found. Thomas doubted whether the Morgans of Brynhir would be able to help them in their inquiry, but he knew the family and was relishing the interview between Peci Brynhir and the inspector. Inspector Evans had several villages in his command and could not know the eccentricities of all the inhabitants. Thomas was a Cilhendre boy and knew all about Peci.

It was hot work following the dusty, dry, rutted cart track that led to the farm. Evans was hoping that they might be offered a drop of something when they arrived. If it was only small beer it would be welcome, even milk, at a pinch. They walked most of the way in silence. Thomas couldn't think of anything to say and the inspector was not much of a one for small talk. They paused at the top of the fourth field and looked back at the village.

"Terrible place to carry a coffin," said Thomas, at last.

Inspector Evans plugged on, walking a yard or so ahead. He had no desire to discuss an undertaker's problems with Thomas. Thomas let him gain on him. The Inspector was therefore the first to reach the stream over which a bridge led into Brynhir farmyard. He found that there was a gate at the bridge, barring his way, and that this gate was padlocked. He shook the gate and suddenly a window rattled up in the farm. A loud voice shouted, in Welsh, words which Evans could not believe. He spoke Welsh but preferred not to let it be known that he suffered from this disability. He raised his head to the farm, his hand still on the gate. The words were repeated.

"Come one step nearer and there's a shot in your arse."

He saw that an upstairs window in the farm was open. A woman crouched at it with a large rifle pointing at the inspector's middle. Fierce dogs growled in the yard.

"My good woman," he shouted, "put that thing away. It might be loaded. Stop playing the fool, I want to speak to you."

There was a cackle of laughter. The voice said, "Loaded, is it?" and a wood pigeon that had been sailing above Evans' head was suddenly lying in the water at his feet while small thunder echoed round the hills.

It was then that Thomas came up, trying not to show his abundant secret joy.

"What's the matter, sir?"

"Matter? Matter? Don't stand there like a dope. Climb over this gate and tell these people that I want to see them."

"No, not I, sir. I wouldn't dare, honest. Peci would shoot me for sure. I'd be a lovely target."

"Damn. What is the meaning of this?"

"Oh, Peci is always like this, sir, she don't like men."

The harsh, incredible voice spoke again.

"W'at you want, Thomas Police? Go from by here or I'll start tellin' you your 'istory. Police, indeed, nothin' but two long legs and nothin' between them. Go from my sight."

"'Spector wants to talk to you, Peci, private."

"I know enough about privates, thank you. Go now, I say, or you'll have a shot in yours. I'm warnin' you, you old broom-stick."

"It's no good, sir, she won't let us in. P'raps you could ask from here. You'll have to talk Welsh, though. She won't answer English."

"You'll answer English, my man, for bringing me up here without a word of what to expect. What's her name?"

"Peci, of course."

"I know that, idiot, Peci what?"

"Duw Mawr, I'm not sure myself. Peci Brynhir I've always called her."

"Useless again. Mistress," said Evans, "if you won't let us in, can you tell us whether you saw anything of Mr. Nixon the manager or anybody else down by the river on the night before last?"

"That dirty pig? No. Have you lost him?"

"He's dead, mistress."

It was hard to shout dead into the hot afternoon. The word echoed round and round the byres. The dogs answered the echoes.

"Serve him right. Dirty old thing, ych a fi. No, I didn't see him, or he might be dead sooner. Be off with you now and don't come back. I got my gun on you, quick, now. March."

And the big voice broke into The March of the Men of Harlech. The inspector was slow to leave until another shot bounced in the dust on the bridge.

"Come on, sir, she means it. She does no harm till you get to her property and then she says you are trespassing. We better go, indeed."

"But this is outrageous. I'll have her prosecuted. Is there no man or somebody with a bit of sense in that place that we could talk to? And you – damn you – you must have known. Why the hell was I not warned?"

"Well, indeed, I thought p'raps she'd open the gate, seeing it was you. Yes, she's got two sons but she keeps the money, so they have to do like they're told."

"Is the woman mad?"

"No, not to say mad. Only a bit funny about men, like. When her husband died, oh, many years ago, some of the chaps round about thought they'd go courtin' Peci, because he left her pretty well off, see? Quite a few went there and pestered her a bit, like, but Peci'd had enough with one and she packed them all off. They didn't leave her in peace whatever, and that's why she put that lock on the gate and keeps the gun handy. They say she has it in bed with her. She got a licence all right, because of the foxes."

The inspector rumbled and thundered down the mountain in the hot afternoon, his uniform dark and tight on his back, cursing the farmers, the village, the strikers, the policemen who were no help to him. Red and breathless, he snarled at Thomas.

"What time does Williams the Road finish work?"

"About four, I think. He starts at six these hot days, I know."

"It's almost four now. We'll go to Williams' at once."

"Yes, sir."

"It will be very enjoyable to talk to a public servant after that woman. At least he is bound to know his place and will treat The Force with the respect it deserves."

"Oh, yes, for sure. He's a tidy man, old Williams. Very great in the chapel."

"No mad women there, I hope."

"No, indeed, sir, there's only Abel, poor fellow, but he's quiet enough. Only religious mania he's got. Been put away once, but his mother couldn't be without him – he's back now. Big family they are too. Let me see, now. There's Ebenezer, Zorobabel, Jonah, Abel, Rachel, Eliazer, Samuel, Malachi and Shadrach."

Thomas was counting on his fingers.

"Ten, and one married."

"Are those their real names?"

"Yes, of course."

"My God! What's the old man's name then?"

"Abraham. His wife is called Polly, but they don't like to say. There's the house, down there, look, sir. Lovely garden. Got a monkey tree and all, the only monkey tree in Cilhendre. We won't be long now."

Big and important, the inspector walked up to the front door of the house. A big sweeping branch of the monkey tree knocked his helmet to one side. He stamped his feet in a fury, but, turning back to blame Thomas for the mishap, he saw that, on the rebound, the tree had caught the taller Thomas in the face. This soothed him. They knocked several times at the front door, but got no reply.

"Better go round to the back. I don't think they ever use this door, sir." The inspector was not in favour of back doors. They robbed one of importance, but he reluctantly consented to try the back door after two more fruitless hammerings at the front. As they turned the corner of the house towards the back, they began to understand why their knocking had gone unheeded. The back door stood open and a considerable amount of jumbled noises came through it. No one feels very confident knocking at an open door and Evans felt as if he were committing sacrilege against his own august self.

It was the daughter of the house, Rachel, who saw them standing there. She was carrying out a wooden tub of dirty water; staggering with the tub raised only about a foot from the ground, her arms stretched full out to take both handles, her bottom high in the air. She saw their feet first and dropped the tub with a jerk, water swung up and out over their clean police boots. She pushed her red hair up from her bird-beak face and said, "Oh, come in. Mind the tub."

They inched past it and took a few steps into the kitchen, while she staggered on, to empty the dirty water away outside. The kitchen was a big room, but it seemed to overflow with people and noise. There were two tables, one at each end of the room, with the fire in between. Seated at the head of the first table, beside the window, was a frail, chestnut haired youngish young man. There was a Family Bible on the table before him. He was reading aloud from the Book of Revelations. "And he had in his right hand seven stars:

and out of his mouth went a sharp two-edged sword and his countenance was as the sun shineth in his strength."

Sitting opposite Abel, at the other end of the scrubbed table, was his brother, Malachi, with a hymn book. He was washed and looked scrubbed, but was dressed only in his flannel shirt and knee-length flannel pants, tied at the knee with tape. He it was who set the note for the singing in chapel, and he was practising in his tenor voice for that night's prayer meeting. A third brother was standing in front of the fire, drying himself after his bath in the wooden tub. He was quite naked but carefully draped a coarse sacking towel around his front. That quite a lot could be seen from behind did not seem to occur to him. His brother, Eli, was still in pit trousers and working boots, waiting for fresh water for his bath. The water boiled in large buckets on the fire.

Shadrach, the dandy of the family, was on strike, so he had no need to bath. He was holding a kitchen chair before him in an attitude of great deference; he waltzed round and round, partnering the chair, in about four square feet of floor, oblivious to everything but the tune of the Blue Danube which he was whistling, to keep time.

In the far corner, by the door to the stairs, two more of the sons were holding, and arguing over, a seed catalogue. They were both keen gardeners and were planning, with threats, what they should plant next year.

Old Williams himself was sitting at the head of the far table, talking to two people who seemed, by their politeness, to be visitors. He was giving an account, with the titles of each sub-section, of the sermon preached last week at the Big Meeting in Bethania. He and the visitors were drinking broth out of pudding basins. Steam rose from the basins as much as from the visitors. Mrs. Williams sat at the other end of the table, cutting up towers of bread and piling food before the poor visitors who were choked with hysteria and too afraid of their voices to risk refusing.

The policemen stood, just over the threshold, when Rachel came back with the empty tub.

"Excuse me, will you?"

She pushed past them and, setting the tub before the fire, she poured into it the water which had been heating. There was a great noise of water and steam rose in a cloud. Cold water was added and Eli, the last to bath, modestly got on with the job of public bathing. He and two brothers were colliery officials, shotsmen, and they were still at work.

Through the mist of steam, Rachel might have been observed shaking her father's sleeve. She shouted in his face: "The policeman wants somethin' – by the door."

"Ask him in girl, ask him in."

Williams got up and motioned to the policemen to come to the table. He seated them opposite the visitors on the only vacant chairs (except for the chair that was waltzing), and before the inspector had answered that, yes, indeed it was a nice day if rather warm, basins of broth had been put before them and they were encouraged to eat. Large hunks of bread were bestowed upon them and before he could get anywhere near his errand, the inspector found himself forced to drink boiling broth at four-fifteen on a very hot August afternoon.

Broth, when very hot, is noisy stuff to drink, but in that Babel the embarrassing sounds were drowned and the inspector decided to accept the situation with as good a grace as was in him to muster. He took his broth with as much elegance as the limiting factors afforded but elegance does not really belong with large spoons, big to the mouth, and pudding basins very full of very hot broth.

When the broth and the bread were finished, Mrs. Williams gave them cups of tea and apple tart, ignoring refusals, as though they were empty forms of behaviour which she had, just now, no time to honour. Feeding callers at the house was a point of honour. Conversation was not exactly flowing.

Mr. Williams went on with his shouted account of last week's sermon and the others cat-listened and nodded. Mrs. Williams was too busy watching for empty plates to contribute more than: "Make yourself at home. Come on. Pitch in. There's plenty more."

There were background noises from Revelations, Mr. Cuthbert's advice to gardeners, "Show me the way to go home", "Where's the soap?", "Drat this cat", and great sloshings of water.

When honour was satisfied and old Williams the Road was toying with another famous preacher, the inspector shouted a whisper that they would like a word with the old man somewhere a bit more private.

"Yes, yes, come you. We'll go down the garden."

Williams led the way to the back door and the policemen, picking up their helmets, threaded after him. It was good to get out into the fresh air and give their ears a rest.

"Lovely garden we got, isn't it? There's a handsome cabbage for you."

"Yes, Mr. Williams, one of the best I've seen this year."

"It's yours, sir, you shall have it."

And Williams was off back to the house, like a little fox. He returned immediately with a gleaming knife in his hand and before Evans had fully realised what was afoot, the large green cabbage was cut and in his arms. Evans felt that this bouquet was not congruous with his dignity nor was it convenient for the coming interview, and, having seen several slugs nestling in the leaves, he passed the cabbage to Thomas to hold for him. But, whip, Thomas was already holding his own cabbage. Evans piled one on top of the other and Thomas could just see daylight over the top.

"Now, there's onions for you, look."

Half a dozen came up and were balanced on top of the cabbage. When several earthy carrots had been added with a speed which quite defied the inspector, old Williams darted off to pick flowers.

"No, no. I've got plenty, no need to refuse, the more you give the more you get in this old world, especially sweet peas. I'll tell you a wrinkle. Empty the pot on sweet peas every morning, that's what they like, but keep the secret, don't tell."

P.C. Thomas was now almost invisible. Only the tip of his helmet showed above the vegetables. Carrot leaves were tickling his ears, the overpowering smell of onions was making his eyes cry; a slug had crept out of the cabbage, and was slowly struggling up his coat sleeve, leaving a silver trail that shone like a rainbow. He looked like a walking market.

Williams came back clutching a large bunch of flowers, hydrangeas, roses, sweet peas, antirrhinums, marigolds, all jumbled up, anyhow, with different stems and different lengths and impossible to hold properly. Inspector Evans sighed, for even he could see that Thomas was too occupied to find room for flowers. The inspector took them and the bull by the horns.

"Thank you, Mr. Williams. Now what we've come about is this. Can you tell us whether you noticed anything at all unusual on the road where the manager was found when you were sweeping there yesterday morning?"

"Well, now. Let me think. Sit down, sir, on this wheelbarrow, look. Put the flowers on the pigsty roof. There now. Are you all right, Glyndwr?" A muffle emerged from the vegetables which was taken to mean that Glyndwr Thomas was quite content. The slug had now reached his elbow.

"Now, what was you asking? Anything unusual on the road by the bridge. No there wasn't nothing much. Let me think, now. Yesterday morning, you said, yesterday morning, now. Oh, aye, of course, that was when I found the cap.

I remember now. There was a cap on the road, but it didn't fit any of ours. I'll show you."

And he was off again up the garden path like a cock robin.

"This may be a clue, Thomas. Wait now. Hold everything."

"I am, worse luck."

He was choked with leaves, which was just as well, perhaps. Williams was back with a tweed cap in his hand.

"Here it is, look. P'raps it will fit you, Glyndwr, you got a big head."

"Let me see it, Williams, at once, man. This is important."

"Oh, is it?"

"My god, it's Mr. Nixon's cap. It's to match his plusfours. Where was it man, quick?"

"On the paving it was. Near all that blood I had to scrub with my brush."

"Blood? Did you say blood?"

"Yes. It's all this drinkin' and fightin'. The men come out of that House of Sin, that Black Horse, the devil's own house, and only say a word wrong with some of them and it's hammer and tongs, 'Go on, Dai, give it to him,' chuffin' and threatenin', and who has to clear up the mess in the morning? Me, poor old Williams the Road. Sick, there is sometimes, too. It's a scandal, that's what it is. I have to carry water from one of the houses to wash it away down the drain. Not right. Parish Council don't take no notice, Roads and Bridges won't take no notice. They ought to make Maggie wash it herself. She has the profit."

"Yes, yes all right, but where was this blood?"

"Well, where I'm sayin'. On the paving by the bridge."

"We'll have to ask you to come with us to show us exactly where it was; and to sign a statement at the Station. I'll be keeping this cap."

"Oh, all right then. Wait while I get my hat and coat. I hope the cap fits, I'm sure."

And Williams was off again up the garden path.

"Do you see what this means, Thomas?"

But Thomas' voice was full of leaves. The slug was making steady progress.

"If that was blood on the road, and if it was Nixon's blood, it means that he was probably attacked on the road and carried down to the river. That would account for the cuts and bruise. A blow on the chin that hit him down on to the road. Hit the curb, perhaps, to get that cut. Then he'd be carried to the river and his head put under water. Suicide, indeed. Now listen to me. You came off duty at eleven, didn't you? Answer, man, can't you?"

Another mumble emerged from among the cabbage.

"Right. At eleven-fifteen then, I would say he was still alive, probably. No one would risk anything till you were off duty. Mrs. Nixon tells me that he left the house at about 10.30. I was there myself until after ten. Right how long does it take to walk from his house to Mafeking, by the round about route? Quarter of an hour? Twenty minutes? Say he get to Mafeking at 10.45 or 10.50 how long would he stay?"

Thomas could not give a reasonable answer, but his ears were blushing behind the carrot tops.

"Twenty minutes or half an hour, perhaps, He would not stay long enough to risk seeing the woman's husband, I'm sure. Say he left at about 11.15 to 11.30. Now, you say that as you went off duty you saw Jack Look-Out turn up Mafeking Terrace from the Canal Bank. That was about 11.15. He may well have met Mr. Nixon in the street because Mr. Nixon must have come back by the main road or he would not have been found by the bridge. Then you say you saw Joseph Everynight and a group of men going out together to Ty Newydd fields. Would they have to pass the bridge to get there?" The vegetables shook as Thomas denied this.

"Put those damn things down and talk some sense, will you?"

"No, don't put them down, Glyndwr. I'm ready now. Off to go." Williams was back again.

"Come along then. Look sharp."

"Don't forget the flowers, 'spector. Oh, drat, the old sow have eaten some, I'm sorry. Never mind, here's a few more." Three sheaves of gladioli were added to the inspector's bouquet.

They set off back to the bridge through Cilhendre village; old Williams with a fox face bouncing along, the inspector looking like a May Queen and Thomas like a harvest festival. The inspector never knew that that was the occasion on which he earned the inevitable nickname, "Call me early."

When they had considered and meditated over the spot marked X, they took Williams back with them to the Police Station to sign his statement. The statement and the cap were put away under lock and key, and Williams was seen to the door and thanked. While Thomas stood at the front door of the Police Station, watching Williams out of sight, he saw Everynight coming towards him.

"Hullo, Glyndwr, 'spector in?"

"Aye mun. Want to see him?"

"No harm in that is there?"

"No, indeed, come on you in. I'll tell him."

Joe sat in Thomas' office while he waited for the inspector to appear. He sat on the edge of his chair, a small, thin, doggy, sly, little man. He held his cloth cap in his hand and span it round and round on his finger as he waited. It went faster and faster until it fell off and flew into a corner by Thomas' table. Joe was crouched to reach it when the inspector came into the room. This rather put Joe off his stroke.

"Well, have you information for me about Mr. Nixon's movements, Davies?"

"Well," said Joe going to his chair again, "really, it's more about my own movements to tell the truth. But I saw the Manager, certainly."

"Good. I'm glad to see that some of you colliers want to help the police for once."

"Well, sir, it was like this, see. Me and the boys was going fox huntin' that night."

"Yes, I know that. Though why they can't be left to be hunted properly by day is more than I can understand."

"Well, sir, we haven't got horses for a start. No, we go after him quiet in the night and pot him when he comes for his supper."

"Pot him? You mean you shoot?"

"Aye, but you don't have to look so cunnin', Manager wasn't shot. We gets the five shillings for his brush, see, for the sake of the chickens, like."

"All right. Go on."

"Well, now, sorry to be a bit personal, but I have to explain that I suffers from the piles something chronic, and if I don't go every day it's look out tomorrow. Now, I hadn't been all day Tuesday and I wanted to be comfortable while we was waiting for foxy, so down I goes to the garden to try, whatever, before going out.

"Well, I sat by there a goodish bit and in the end, mun, I was all right, but, jawch cried, there was no paper when I went to look. Our kids is terrible; they steal every bit of newspaper they find to take to the chip shop. She gives them a few chips see, for a pile of papers. Well, they must have raided the W for paper and there I was, mun, stuck. We used to have some orange papers there, but not since the strike, and they're too thin for a start. If there's gold paint on them it comes off. Newspaper for me every time, for a read while I concentrate. Well, like I was saying, there wasn't even orange paper left so I opens the door to shout thinkin' somebody would hear me, whatever.

"There I was shoutin' 'Paper, paper,' like one of them boys in Swansea High Street, aye, when who should I see passin' our fence but Manager. There was a good moon and I saw him as plain as my face. I don't think he heard me, he didn't stop, whatever, and in the end I found a few old odds and ends in my pockets and managed that way. That was about quarter to 'leven, because I wanted to hurry to meet the boys at 'leven."

"Where is your house exactly, Davies?"

"Well, the house is in Pentregwynt, but the W is by the Welfare Field, top of the garden, see?"

"The Welfare Field runs behind your garden then?"

"Well, aye, that's what I said. Our W was the Grand Stand for the Carnival. Lovely view from the roof."

"About a quarter to eleven, you said?"

"Aye."

"Have you any idea where Mr. Nixon would be going at that time of night, in that direction?"

"No, can't say I have. There wasn't a football match on," said Everynight, bland.

"You didn't see him after that did you? Later?"

"No."

"Are you sure?"

"Damn, here I am. I've come here to give you information and what thanks do I get for it? Remarks. Well, you can keep your remarks and thank you very much, let me tell you. I'm off."

"Now, now, there's no need to get angry. I'll withdraw that question."

"I should hope so too."

"What were your movements after – after you left your house?"

"By the time I'd got my gun and my few things ready, I was a bit late and I went round the gardens to call all the boys. So we was pretty late starting, all told. Must have been half past, I think."

"Where did you go?"

"Up the Gelli to Ty Newydd fields."

"How did you go?"

"How? Walkin', how d'you think? Pony and trap?"

"No, what route did you take?"

"Oh, we went down Pentregwynt, past the Square, turned right this side of the bridge, past the Doctor's and up to Ty Newydd."

"So you didn't cross the bridge?"

"No."

"Did you see anybody about?"

"Not a pilkin."

"What about the way home? Did you see anybody then?"

"No. We was all too mad at Lewis Jones Baboon, to take a lot of notice. He'd been teachin' spellin' to our fox and we was a bit put off, like. But there was nobody about then, for sure. Be about three or four then."

"Right. Now we want to know who was with you. Give the list to Thomas, here, while I draw out a statement for you to sign from my notes."

"All right. Are you ready Glyndwr?"

"Yes. Right now. Not too quick."

"There was me, for one."

"Yes."

"Lewis Jones Baboon."

"I can't write Baboon on Police Reports, mun."

"Well, put it in blacklead and rub it out after."

"Aye. Right. Who else?"

"Will Jones Swank, Joseph Jones Grannie, Jim Lewis Fullpelt, Jack Irish – what's his name? Something like Dewer – I don' know. He talks so funny, mun."

"Wait a minute. I got it by here somewhere. He had to have a permit to work because of the Free State. Here it is, mun – John Mary O'Dwyer."

"O'Dwyer – well, myn uffern i. Nice to know, whatever. Did you say his name was Mary? Funny name to give a chap, too."

"Who else, Joe?"

"Tom All Baba and Elwyn Jeffries Jess. That's all."

"Elwyn was with you was he?"

"Yes."

"Wait a bit now, to sign your name for the inspector."

"When's the inquest, Glyndwr?"

"Friday morning. Funeral in the afternoon."

"Keepin' him long, this weather too. He'll be calling for the earth by then, drop dead. There's a slug on your collar, Glyndwr. Come here for me to take it off."

"Ta."

"Marked your coat too. Pity."

"Look out, here he comes."

"Sign this please, Davies. Read it first, man. Have you given that list to Thomas?"

"Yes."

"Well, thank you, Davies. It was public spirited of you to come."

"That's all right, inspector. So long."

"Good evening."

"So long, Glyndwr."

"So long. Sir, look at this list. Elwyn Jeffries was out with them. That makes him safe."

"Yes. If Davies is telling the truth. We'll check up on that right away. You will call on all those people and get independent lists. Ask them all what route they took. They may have done quite a lot of dirty work long before they turned to Ty Newydd fields. I'm not so curious about their return journey because I feel sure the crime was committed early in the night – where would he have spent the time, if you take it that he was killed after midnight? He wouldn't want to risk meeting that woman's husband. Perhaps he did meet him, Thomas. I wonder. I must go and see those two right away."

"Yes, sir."

"You set off now, at once."

Thomas's feet were sore, he had a corn on his middle toe, and he was longing to paddle in a nice warm bowl with Epsom Salts in the water, but the inspector wasn't a man to understand about corns and Thomas put on his helmet again.

"While you check that list, I'll see the Jeffries crowd and Jack Morris, since they live in the same direction."

"Yes, sir."

CHAPTER 11

Jess Jeffries had spent the day indoors. She buried her head in the housework; making a mountain of Welsh cakes, baking bread, telling the children all the stories she could remember, Tarzan of the Apes and Sinbad the Sailor, Moses in the Bulrushes. She talked with gush and flourishes and thumped the dough as though it owed her rent. She laughed too loud at the children and brushed their hair too hard. Her fears were gnawing like maggots; her greatest terror was that the chapel deacons would bring her case before the members and have her publicly cut out of the chapel. That and the whisperings in the village. That her husband might be accused of murder, perhaps hanged seemed too remote a possibility, too unlike what life meant for her. But the chapel was a reality and its laws much nearer home than the Law of Judge and Jury.

She heard the cryer shout his message at the bottom of the street and was prompted to put the bread in the tins for the dough had risen enough. She made no other responses to the cryer but she could hear the neighbours talking after his departure. Were they talking about her? Wondering if she would go to the old police? Well, she wouldn't, so there. As the afternoon wore on she began to feel more secure and her gestures were less exaggerated. She hardly thumped the cups at all when she laid the tea table.

She was washing the children for bed. She set them, in vests and knickers, to sit on the kitchen table while she rubbed them with soap and a piece of flannel. The two younger ones were clean and in their nightdresses, the third playing with lather in the bowl, when the inspector called.

She answered the door, drying her hands on her apron. She was almost relieved to see that it was the inspector and not the minister.

She showed him into her parlour, full of three piece and china cabinet.

"Will you sit down for a minute, till I finish the children?"

"Yes, of course, Mrs. Jeffries, you go along. I'll wait."

Jess rushed to the kitchen, finished washing the children and quickly sent them upstairs.

"I'll bring your supper up to bed when this man's gone. Behave now and don't quarrel."

She went back to the parlour, shy and uncomfortable. Inspector Evans was sitting back at his ease in an armchair, his head resting on a satin cushion. She hoped he wasn't wearing old oil on his hair. She tried not to be overawed by the policeman; he was a friend of the Manager's; all men were the same, posh or not, no need to be nervous.

"Now, Mrs. Jeffries, I wonder if you'll answer a few questions for me, please. You will see that I have come here – on my own so that you and I can talk more privately. I will try to keep as much as possible of what you tell me from becoming public knowledge. I understand that you were a friend of Mr. Nixon's and I am trying to find out where he went on the night that he was killed. I'm sure that you are as anxious as I am to find out who harmed him. He was a good friend to me too and I shall miss him."

Jess said nothing; she went on pleating and pleating her apron. So the police did know. Did everybody then?

"Tell me, Mrs. Jeffries, did you see him on the night he was killed?"

"I don't know anything about him." Her lips were closed thin.

"Oh, come, come, Mrs. Jeffries. You wouldn't deny that you were friendly with him."

No cockerel crew as Jess said, "I don't know nothing, I tell you."

"From information received we think he came here that night. We can call the person who informed us to give evidence at the inquest. It would all come out then in open court. Co-operate with us now, and we may be able to save everyone a great deal of trouble."

"Oh, there's lies. He wasn't here. You can ask Elwyn, we were both of us at home. The two of us."

"Your husband was at home then?"

"Yes."

"Is he at home then?"

"No. He's gone up the mountain for sticks, but he won't be long."

"So he was at home with you on Tuesday night?"

"Yes. I've told you twice."

"You surprise me, Mrs. Jeffries. I was under the impression that he had gone for foxes with Joseph Davies. But Joseph may have made a mistake, of course."

"Joseph – ? Who? Oh, Everynight. Yes, of course. Perhaps I've mixed things up a bit. What night did you say?"

"Tuesday, Mrs. Jeffries, the night before the carnival."

"Oh, yes, sorry. Elwyn was out, out with those boys. I remember now. And I was by myself in the house. I went to bed early."

"Are you quite sure now? Perhaps Mr. Nixon called and you've forgotten that too."

"No, no he never. I don't know anything about him."

"Somebody says that he saw Mr. Nixon at your back door that night."

"Well he's tellin' lies, then, cheeky thing."

"All right then, Mrs. Jeffries. We'll leave it there for now. You may remember more by tomorrow. There'll be an inquest, as I said, that will be on Friday and we may have to call you as a witness. You'll be on your oath then."

"I don't care," she lied, only her big dark eyes telling the truth. For a moment Evans understood his friend as he looked into those naked eyes. He was still angry with Mrs. Nixon. He picked up his helmet.

"I'm sorry, Mrs. Jeffries, that you can't help us," his hand on the knob of the door. "Think it over and I'll call again, some time tomorrow. Good night, now."

"So long."

The inspector let himself out. As he opened the front door he saw that there was a plate behind it; on the plate was a fine piece of fresh salmon, keeping cool on the flags. There was a clean bit of thin butcher's muslin over it. He thought that the manager must have paid very well for his pleasures. He and Mrs. Evans could never rise to more than a small tin of John West.

Jess did not move. She sat on in her chair, her thoughts like rabbits chased by ferrets. She bit the nail on her little finger and rubbed her face to rub out the trouble. Had she done right about Elwyn? Who could have seen him by the back door? Could they move away to live? Could she have a doctor's paper not to go to their old inquest? Oh, God, give me some help, will you?

"Our Mam," said a small voice at the door. "Can we have our supper now? We saw the man going. Mrs. Thomas next door was on the door when he went. Is he taking us to jail?"
"Oh, sorry, lovie. Mam forgot. No, no. Nobody's going to jail. Never you worry. I'll bring your supper up in a wink and a sweet each for being quiet."

"What's the matter, Mam, why are you talkin' so loud?"

"Nothing, love, nothing. Go on you to bed now, there's a good girl. I won't be a minute."

It was only a short walk to Jack Morris Look-Out's house from Jess Jeffries', unless you needed to walk quietly, in the shadows. The inspector had come on foot, thinking that the Rover would make too great a sensation, and you never knew what the kids in Mafeking Terrace wouldn't do to a car if it was left on its own. Try to drive it, like as not; blow the horn, for sure. He thought that by coming on foot he was making a tactful gesture, but his presence in the street was as big as a summons. Jack Morris was trying to persuade himself that Evans could have no reason for coming to see him.

Jack and his neighbour, Tommy, were together in the street when they sighted him.

"Look out, here he comes. What the hell were we talkin' about, Tommy? Say something till he's passed whatever."

"Lovely evening now, isn't it, Jack? If this weather lasts water will be short. I hear the farmers want to pray for rain." Tommy's voice was off-key.

"Oh, do they?" said Jack, falsetto and false. Then under his breath in his own voice, "I wish the buggers would pray for me."

"Aye, so Jones the deacon was telling me."

"Christ, say something else."

"Did you enjoy the carnival, boy? Old Cow-and-Gate was a riot, wasn't he, mun, with them bones and all. Fair play to Mairwen too. Her costume was better than mine, but in reverse. No defeatism about her, oh no."

"Look out, here we go."

"Morris, can I have a few words with you, please?"

"Yes."

"I'd like to ask you some questions, in private."

"Tommy, by here, can hear anything you got to ask me."

"Very well. I want to know your movements on Tuesday night of this week, from about ten-thirty onwards please."

"Tuesday did you say?"

"Yes, the night before the carnival."

"Oh, aye. That was the night we was playin' dominoes, wasn't it, Tommy?"

"Aye, come to think, that's right. We was talkin' about w'at to wear. We played dominoes till all hours. I can't sleep much with my old chest, see, Inspector, and Jack, by here, do keep me a lot of company."

"When did you start playing?"

"Be about ha' past ten, wouldn't it Jack?"

"About that, aye."

"Then how, Morris, do you account for the fact that you were seen by a reliable witness, at the bottom of this street, turning up from the canal bank at about 11.10 that night?"

"Well, he must have made a mistake, mustn't he?"

"You are not on oath now, either of you. But I want you to try and remember more exactly when that game of dominoes began. Davies, remember that if you give false evidence in a murder case, you can be accused of being an accessory after the fact. It would be a long stretch."

"Damn you, what are you sayin'? Tommy is no accessory to no murder. I haven't committed no murder, and look out if you say that again, copper or no."

"I didn't say so, Morris. But you were known to be no friend of Mr. Nixon's and you deny being outside that night. Let me tell you that you were seen by a member of the police force, coming down from the canal bank and turning up this street. There was a good moon, you may remember and my witness was standing on the Square, not seventy yards away."

"Well, tell him he needs his eyes tested."

"Davies, will you take your oath that Morris was with you at eleven o'clock that night?"

"No, he won't. I wasn't with him. But I didn't kill Nixon. I'd been somewhere on my own business, nothing to do with you, and I was in bed by ha' past eleven."

"I'll have more information than that, my lad. Better come

to the Station now and make a proper statement. Come quietly, without a fuss."

"No damn fear. If you want me, you get a summons. I won't go quiet and it'll take a better man than you to drag me there."

"Very well. If that's the way you want it, that's the way you'll get it. I'll see you again, my lad."

"I'm not your bloody lad, see?"

The inspector walked away exultant. Things were moving. He would have something to report to the Chief Constable in Brecon. No one could say that Inspector Ernest Evans was not up to his job. He decided to round off his interviews with a visit to the magistrate to get the summonses signed. He decided to take his car to D.J.'s house and went back to the Police Station where he had left it.

At the station, Thomas was back, agog.

"Did you see those men, Thomas?"

"Yes, sir. And I found something out."

"Did you? What?"

"I went round to all those chaps on Joe's list and everyone of them who was on that procession last night said Elwyn Jeffries was with them on the hunt. But Joseph Jones Grannie scalded his foot, making tea, and he didn't go on the march; he said Elwyn wasn't with them. At least, he didn't name him in his first list to me. I asked him if there was anybody else. Are you sure? Of course I'm sure, think I'm blind, he said. Then I asked if he knew where Elwyn Jeffries was. He looked a bit surprised at that and gave me a very old-fashioned look, then he said, jawch, I believe Elwyn was there too, come to think. Now, I believe —"

"Yes. I can see what you're thinking. They decided during that randyboo of theirs to give Jeffries an alibi and forgot that this other chap wasn't with them. And, like the fools they are, they didn't warn him. Good for you, Thomas, you're waking up in your old age. Think they can make a fool of me, do they? They'll see, they'll see. I'll get them, the whole pack of them. They're probably all in it. Giving alibis left, right and centre. I'll alibi them, just you watch. Oh boy! Where's my car? I'm going to D. J. Williams' house. I'll give them alibis. Did you hear anything about that child on your rounds? It sticks in my throat, that baby. I feel in my bones there's a connection somewhere, if we could only see it. You can go home now, Thomas. Wilkins, stay in the office till I get back with the summonses. I'll get them drawn out now."

"Yes, sir."

"Goodnight, then, sir."

CHAPTER 12

After his rest on Thursday morning, D. J. Williams was kept occupied with the small busyness of death, the undertaker, the minister, the insurance, the wreaths, the relations. That evening, after an early supper, he and his mother were sitting together, D.J. still at the table, making patterns in the crumbs and his mother at the fireside, nursing her cat, Brit.

"What's troubling you most, Davy?"

"Most, Mam fach? I don't know for sure; I think about Gwen, she was so young, so much promise. And I've got so much else on my mind that I can't think enough about her. I'm not paying any real respect to the dead, me with my wreaths and my thoughts on other things. Feel guilty.

"She's died young and innocent, like a girl in a poem; and the Manager, he's in a story, too, in a way. You feel that it's so right for him to die a violent death that it can't be true. Right for the novels, right for the Bad Man.

"Pity for him, too. He wasn't all bad, I suppose. It must be awful to feel that nobody will care much when you go. It's a bit like thinking you know there's no Heaven. Certainly no immortality in the thoughts of someone who loved you. No, I wouldn't like that a bit. And who would really like to see him again? His mother, perhaps, remembering him when he was a baby, but I can't picture him in napkins, somehow."

"Don't blaspheme, Davy Williams, for shame."

Ann, with rheumatic, work-worn hands, went on stroking her cat who purred like an engine and voluptuously dug in and sucked out his claws on Ann's knees.

"But what's worrying me most is the murderer. Who can he be, Mam? and how is he feeling now? God knows, I'm

112

sorry for him; he's probably a Cilhendre boy, someone we know.

"And whoever buried the baby will be worrying too. Everything is so sordid.

"I'm a terrible magistrate, Mam, I see these things as results before I realize they are crimes. I begin to see why too soon. I should never have gone on the Bench. Can you bear it, Mam?" he smiled.

"I'll put up with you, I suppose. The elbow is nearer than the wrist." Davy drew shapes on the cloth with the prongs of his fork.

"If they catch whoever did it they'll hang him, Mam, and the Manager didn't lead a good life."

"Are you saying you don't want them to catch him?"

"Don't say things so baldly," he said, putting down the fork with minute care. "I don't know really what I want. As a magistrate, I want the crime to be punished – though I don't know how it ought to be punished; as an ordinary, sensible man I want everyone but the murderer cleared of suspicion, but as a Christian I think of forgiving seventy times seven and as Davy Williams, native of Cilhendre, collier, I suspect I'd like him to get away with it. And did you ever hear such talk from a man who's supposed to be a Justice of the Peace – even if he has been in jail?"

"But, Davy, the Lord said 'Thou shalt not kill.'"

"You say that to the hangman then. If he is caught I'll be in part responsible, and if he is hanged, therefore, it follows that I'll be in part responsible for that too. It's all the way, if you begin a thing, see." He pushed his chair away from the table and, standing, said, in a kind of bottled voice, "But I don't believe in hanging. What good has it ever done? The strike was bad enough, and people hungry, but this as well. Remember me reading Hamlet? – I read out that bit to you about 'the times are out of joint' – well there it is, out of joint like rheumatic, and hungry as well."

Ann shook her head and got out of her chair, putting Brit on the cushion. "Oh well, this won't earn the old woman her ninepence. I better clear the table." She piled the cups and saucers together. "Davy, are you worried about the baby too?"

"Oh well, that's a small crime, in my eyes, to save some poor girl's name, no doubt. The baby was stillborn. It's only the regulations about registering births and deaths that have been broken. There's no question of any foul play, according to the doctor. Inspector Evans wants to connect the two, but that's because he's sort of melodramatic."

"If it would help you at all, I know a bit about the baby." Ann was relieved to find a legitimate excuse to unburden herself of the secret which she knew she would be driven sometime to tell Davy. It was too uncomfortable to live in the same house without sharing a secret.

"What did you say?"

"I know whose the baby was. But it's a secret, remember. I'm not telling D. J. Williams, J.P., only Davy."

"All right. Who is it, Mam?"

"Gwen."

"Gwen? Gwen next door?"

"Yes."

"But she's been in bed for months."

"That's why nobody knew."

"What about the doctor?"

"Well, I'm not sure; he's a dark horse, but he's old now, and perhaps he only looked at her chest, and she wasn't much bigger than a mole hill. I think it arrived a bit too soon and the birth was quick. When it was dead born I suppose they decided to hide everything."

"Is that why she died?"

"No, she was sure to go. She died of the decline and sorrow. It was a terrible death, Davy. She was afraid to the very end. Afraid and yet knowing that it was coming. I've heard people say they were dying many times but with her I suddenly saw in her eyes that she knew it was true, that it wasn't just a thing to say any more. It wasn't very nice, my boy. I wish people would think more about the New Testament, I'm not very fond of the Old, save me from saying so."

"But, Mam, Gwen hadn't got a sweetheart had she?"

"Not that I knew of, but I didn't ask, of course. That had nothing to do with me or with anybody else."

"No, I know, but it would be interesting to know, all the same. I can see now why Gerwin's been so funny lately. I thought it was – because she was so ill, and because he was on strike at such a time, but the other must have been on my mind even more, I think. Was it Gerwin buried the baby then?"

"Yes, but I didn't ask any more. Don't show them that you know, Davy. It's a big secret. They wouldn't like you to know because it would put you in an awkward position with Inspector."

"Why did you tell me, then?"

"It's different if I tell you, as long as they don't know you know."

"Logic! No I won't say anything, but I wonder whether he did see anything that night. Anything to do with the Manager, I mean."

"Well, you can't ask him now."

"No. I shouldn't be surprised if the Inspector calls tonight. He's bound to want to see me soon."

"Mind, then, let me finish clearing this table. Though how he'll have the face to come after putting you in his old jail, I don't know."

"We won't say anything about Gwen to him. He's got the murder on his mind." Ann went to the back door to shake out the cloth.

"If they don't find out who did it, Mam, innocent people may be suspected for years, that's the trouble. People away from Cilhendre who don't know us will blame the strikers, perhaps say it's part of a plan of violence. People are so soft and so ready to pass judgement, especially when they understand least. Some think we are all desperate, violent men in the pits, like black savages from Africa, queer people who vanish under the ground like devils or goblins. They do, honest, don't laugh. When I was in Ruskin College I sometimes felt people treating me with interested kindness and looking at me like a specimen from strange lands, brought over for their scientific curiosity. Made me feel like a thing in a Wild Beast Show, I wondered whether to talk or growl. Both would surprise them equally."

"You and your fancies. You're too sensitive, Davy bach."

"Yes, Yes, I know.

"If the police don't solve this thing, the whole community will be held responsible by some people. They won't have coal for their fires and their factories and then they'll say it's the fault of the colliers who won't do an honest day's work – who go about murdering people and getting away with it.

"But if they catch him it won't bring Nixon back to life. This is it, of course. When you take something on, you think of the honour and the opportunity, the dignity, never of the paying. D. J. Williams, J.P., sounds good, but capital punishment and corporal punishment – I never thought enough. I never dreamed a situation like this would crop up. I'll have to resign from the Bench of course; pity, too. I like part of it."

"Well you can start tidying up your mind a bit, my boy, Inspector is coming through the gate. I'll go next door out of the way. Good evening Inspector. Come in. Yes, Davy's in here. I'll slip out for a minute, excuse me."

"Good evening, Mrs. Williams, don't let me disturb you."

"No, it's all right, I want to see how they are next door before I go to bed."

"Come in, Inspector, come in. Oh, you don't like cats do you? I'll put Brit in the back kitchen. Just a minute. You sit down."

"Thank you. No, I was never much of a one for cats."

Davy carried out the cat and tried to patch himself up before returning to the policeman. He held Brit, warm and fat and silky and sleepy, for a few moments while he tried to weed out some of his more outrageous sentimentalities. "All right," he whispered, "we'll manage. Be wise, pussy, be wise now." Armoured and acting efficient, Davy returned.

"You are looking rather pleased, Inspector. Have you heard good news?"

"I think we are getting somewhere, Mr. Williams. I've come to ask you to sign these summonses for the inquest on Friday."

"Have you got far with your investigations, Inspector?"

"Well, indeed, Mr. Williams, I wondered whether you would go over the case with me, if you wouldn't mind. Two heads, like. That is, if you wouldn't mind, of course."

"No, no, of course not," D.J. lied, "anything I can do." The Inspector wriggled his fat bottom more comfortably into Ann Williams' chair and crossed his fat feet in front of him.

"It's nice to find a bit of comfort. I've had a hard day, Mr. Williams. Well, now, as you know, the manager was killed on Tuesday night. I now believe he was killed on the bridge itself. His cap was found on the road there and Williams, the road sweeper, claims that he cleared away a lot of blood stains there on Wednesday morning. He says he thought that men coming from the Black Horse had been fighting and accounted for the blood stains that way."

"Yes, Williams has got strong views about that. He keeps writing to Brecon about it. But even he should have had the sense to realise that not many people in Cilhendre have money left to go and get fighting drunk in these times."

"But you see what this means, don't you? Whoever committed this foul deed carried the body down to the river and hid it by the bridge. Now that suggests a very strong man, or more likely a number of men."

"One frightened man is very strong, Inspector, I've seen men underground move weights, in fear, that you wouldn't dream possible."

"Yes, I'll grant you that. All right, then. I would say, from Williams' evidence, that the murderer hit Mr. Nixon a terrible blow to the chin, a real fourpenny. He was knocked out and fell backwards so that his head smashed against the kerbstone. That would account for the wound on his head and for the bruise on his chin."

"Any hope of making it a manslaughter charge, then? It wasn't the blow that killed him, but the accident of hitting the kerb."

"Did you say hope, Mr. Williams? I know you are on strike and in with these rioters, but I hoped you were still interested in justice."

"Sit down, Inspector, sit down. Don't get excited. You and I must work together, and quarrelling and a lot of old dignity won't help. Of course I said hope. For a start I would rather not think that murder had been committed in Cilhendre. I would rather, for Mrs. Nixon's sake, believe that the manager had died by accident. I don't like to feel that Mr. Nixon in his last hours drove anyone to murder. Think of going to face your Maker in that sort of a mood. He was your friend, you don't want to think anybody hated him so much that they were driven to killing him, do you?"

"But dragging him down to the river and neglecting him there smacks of murder. You can't get away from that."

"Well let's leave that side of it now to the coroner and the inquest. What else did you find out?"

The inspector made a humph noise and pulled his lower lip back in again. He shifted on his chair like a hen on eggs.

"The first things to look for in a criminal investigation are motive and opportunity, Mr. Williams. We seem to have a wide choice of suspects with both. The obvious suspect to my mind is Elwyn Jeffries, Mafeking Terrace. He certainly had both."

"Did he, indeed? But you cannot ignore the factor of personality, man. Can you honestly see Elwyn committing murder? He's one of the gentlest men I know."

"He's been up before the Bench as you know. For poaching salmon in Cray Reservoir, you remember."

"There's a bit of difference between poaching and murder, Evans."

"Well, then, argue these facts away. Facts, mind, not generalisations about a man's temperament. First, I am now inclined to believe that Mrs. Jeffries was in fact Mr. Nixon's er, er —"

"Yes, I heard that."

"There you are. Motive established. Jealous husband. Nothing clearer. Opportunity. Now, this is where the summons is needed. Mrs. Jeffries told me at first that her husband was at home with her on Tuesday night and Mr. Nixon had not been there. Then, when I told her that someone had testified that Elwyn was with him on that night, she changed her tune and said she might have forgotten. But she still maintains that Nixon was not there."

"He may not have been."

"But I know he was. He was followed there by his son who told me himself."

"Dear, dear, and does Mrs. Nixon know too?"

"Yes, of course she does."

"Poor woman, I'm sure she finds it hard to know how to feel." The Inspector made his humph noise again.

"To go back to Jeffries. You may have heard that Joe Davies, who for some reason is called Everynight –"

"That's because he has so many children."

"I'm afraid I still don't see the point, but never mind; this man, Everynight, went out to look for foxes on Tuesday with a party of his cronies. He claims that Jeffries was with him. And so do all the others except one – and that one –" the inspector pointed a finger like a sausage at D.J. – "that one was the only one who stayed home from that demonstration last night. He was at home with a scalded foot while the others were making Jeffries' alibi."

"But, twt y baw, Jeffries wasn't bound to have been murdering the manager. He could have been doing something else – having his own back on Jess perhaps. What does he himself say?"

"I haven't seen him yet. I've been very busy all day and he was out collecting sticks when I saw his wife. I can't do everything," sulkily, like a boy.

"Surely one of the constables could have been to see him? No one expects you to do all the work."

"I would rather do it myself. This is murder, not dog licences, and I want to see everything done right."

"Even at the risk of not doing everything? I would think you'd be better employed asking the man straight out instead of this round and round the mulberry bush technique."

D.J.'s irritation with the inspector was mounting. He knew he could do little good by picking holes, but the omniscience of this bladder of lard was galling him. D.J. was fond of Elwyn Jeffries and it maddened him when Elwyn was turned over and explored like inferior merchandise.

"Go on with your case. Have you more against Elwyn?"

"No, except that he is a strong man and could have pulled the Manager down to the river."

"What about your other suspects?"

"Ah! there's Jack Morris Look-Out."

"What is your case against him?"

"Well, motive first of all. He was heard to say that he would be willing to swing for Mr. Nixon and he wanted to tar and feather him. He seems to have been a sworn enemy of my friend."

"Most of the men in this village have that same motive, Inspector. Now you have no call to look affronted. I know you and the Manager were great friends and you naturally don't want anything said against him, especially since he's dead. But remember, I like Elwyn Jeffries too. Nixon was a hard man to work under."

"Well, if men won't do their work properly they must expect to be told off!"

"Are you suggesting that no one in Cilhendre pit did work properly?"

"If they did there'd be no need of this strike, now, would there?"

"Oh, for Heaven's sake, Inspector, mun. Don't be so superficial. Do you think this strike is Cilhendre's private property? It's nation-wide, man."

"And a disgrace too."

"Look, did you come here to discuss the ethics of striking with me or not? If you did I better put on my collar and tie. But, remember two things, please, Evans, first, I am on strike, and second, I knew Mr. Nixon as one of his workmen. And, thirdly, if you want to know, I was out myself on Tuesday night, come to think. There you are, another suspect. Motive – intense dislike. Opportunity – out on my own on that night."

"What time would that be?"

"Some time in the small hours."

"I don't think you will have seen anything relevant then." The inspector ceased to smell a rat and resumed his confidential tone. "I think he was killed earlier in the night. My view is that he met his murderer when he was leaving the Jeffries house on his way home. He was found between the two houses and I don't think he would stay late with Mrs. Jeffries for fear of meeting her husband – which is what I think he may well have done. Did you see anything when you were out?"

"No. I went for a walk because I couldn't sleep and I walked the mountain. I thought then I had seen something, but it was only an idea, nothing to interest you."

"Nothing to do with Mr. Nixon?"

"No, thank God. It was my way out from all the Mr. Nixons. What else have you against Jack?"

"Thomas, my P.C., saw him coming from the backs of the houses, looking round furtively before turning up to Mafeking Terrace round about eleven o'clock. Thomas was just about to go off duty and he stayed behind a minute or two, just to make sure all was well. Fair play to Thomas, his head is like a sieve, but he tries to do his duty. We reckoned that if he went home then, Jack Look-Out might have passed Mr. Nixon coming from the Jeffries house. But, I must confess that up until this evening I didn't think that was much to go on. I saw him tonight, though, and asked him what his movements were on Tuesday. That man with a cough, Tommy Davies, Morris's neighbour, provided him with an alibi as fast as striking a match, but when I muttered something about Davies being an accessory after the fact, Morris snapped the bait and said, no, that story they had told was not true but that I could mind my own business, etc. I want him summoned for the inquest as well as Mrs. Jeffries so that they can be called on oath."

"Dear, dear, dear, there's muddy water you fish in, don't you? And you are not too particular how you get your answers are you!"

D.J. wondered what it was like always to be suspecting, always turning the penny over to make sure. Poor Inspector, too, no wonder he was that way, living such a nasty sniffing life. Must be like living too close to too many pigsties. Probably why his face was so red, afraid to breathe deep, for the smell, like having the cryer in to tea. After his little private joke, D.J. felt a little better, less tense.

"Who else is on the black list, then?"

"There are those who went to look for the fox. They could all be in it together. And then there's still the baby's body, Mr. Williams. I am not satisfied at all about that; it looked like a perfect clue when we found it so close, but it's taken us no further at all."

"I think it's just coincidence. Not important. You've got enough on your plate as it is."

"But I think this is part of the other."

"I doubt it. I know how you feel. It must have been like Maria Monk or the Mystery of the Red Barn to find the baby and the body, especially when you think of the Manager's reputation. You probably felt dramatic, like the moving pictures, but I'm afraid you'll have to give that bit of drama up and plump for a sordid little murder. A rather unpleasant man who got what he had been asking for, for a long time."

"I'm surprised to hear you talk like this, Mr. Williams. I'm deeply shocked."

"Are you, really, in your heart? We know what you think of strikers, don't we? Don't forget that I am one of them and that I spent last night with one or two of them. It was an interesting experience."

"I'm sorry about that, Mr. Williams."

"Oh, don't say that. You were right, perfectly right. Fully justified. Let's go back to this business. Have you found out anything else?"

"We haven't had very long at our investigations but I don't think we have done badly, do you? We'll have the inquest tomorrow – just the formal evidence of identity and the testimony of these characters. Then we'll ask for an adjournment,

so that we can get the funeral over. I hope the Chief Constable is going to be satisfied. I've had the demonstration
on my hands too, remember."

"I'm not likely to forget. I'm sorry, I shouldn't have said
that. And that is your case so far is it? About the inquest.
Are you calling John Nixon for anything more than the
formal identification? Is all that dirty linen about his father
coming out? And, by the way, since your method of deciding
on suspects is to choose someone with a motive who was
out fairly early that night, what about John himself? What
did he do after following his father? The Lord knows I don't
want to cast any stones, but he seems to qualify too, doesn't
he?"

The inspector sat silent. Of course he hadn't considered
John Nixon. Why consider a good, superior boy like that
when the village was stiff with colliers?

"Twt, twt, Mr. Williams, you're not serious, are you?"

"Why not?"

"You told me to study Elwyn Jeffries' character, why don't
you practise what you preach? John Nixon is a well educated,
well-mannered gentleman and devoted to his mother."

"Yes, Inspector, devoted to his mother. He wouldn't like
anyone to wrong her, would he? He's a sensitive, sympathetic
young man and would know how she must have felt. Of
course, he may have known how his father felt too – would
that make him more or less likely to kill him, I wonder? What
do you think?"

"I haven't thought of it," said Evans, short, and redder in
the face, small purple veins on his nose and cheekbones. "I
won't think of it. It's nonsense. Dangerous nonsense."

"Is it? Perhaps so. Well, it's your job, not mine, thank God.
Give me the summonses will you? Where's my pen now?
Upstairs I'm afraid, in my other suit. Wait you there, excuse
me a minute."

D.J. left the room and climbed the stairs. As he climbed, slowly for his breath, his face was twisted and ugly, as though he had heartburn. He tried not to think, went to his jacket which was hanging in his bedroom and took out his Swan fountain pen. As he unclipped it he looked at the framed text above his bed – "Him that cometh to me, I will in no wise cast out," decorated with purple lilies. "Even the inspector?" he asked and went on again down the stairs.

Left alone in Ann Williams' kitchen, the inspector looked round and stalked to a small mahogany, glass-fronted book-case. He recognised the Dickens and had a passing know-ledge of Shakespearian titles. Browning and Tennyson seemed more than respectable, but who were Norman Angell, Upton Sinclair, D. H. Lawrence? Never heard of any of those.

"You're interested in my books, Inspector? Is there any-thing you'd like to borrow?"

"No, thank you, all the same. I'm so busy I don't seem to have any time for reading. When I do have some leisure I like to play a game of bridge. You don't play, do you, Mr. Williams?"

"No. Nothing against cards, you know, though some of my fellow deacons will tell you they belong to the devil. No, I'd rather read. Each to his taste, of course."

D.J. sat at the table again, spreading out the *Daily Herald* to form a pad for his writing. He glanced through the sum-monses and signed them like Pontius Pilate.

"There you are, then."

"Thank you. I'll have these served tomorrow."

"Pay my respects to the Chief Constable, will you, when you report to him? I haven't seen him since I was last up for the Education Committee."

"Yes, I'll do that, Mr. Williams."

"Have a drop of elderberry before you go. It will strengthen you."

"Thank you. I think I will indeed. Your mother has got the secret of this wine and no mistake. My wife can't make it at all."

"The hard part is keeping it, not making it. It ought to be kept four or five years before it's drunk, but the temptation is very great. Perhaps you are not so tempted as I am. Try it and see. Mam will give Mrs. Evans the recipe."

"Here's your good health."

"And yours."

"Will you say good night to Mrs. Williams for me?"

"Yes, surely. She'll be sorry to have missed you. Good night, now."

"Good night."

The magistrate went to the door with the inspector and then walked quickly through the hedge to the next house, to tell his mother she could leave her sanctuary and to say good night to his neighbours.

CHAPTER 13

Friday was a nice day for the funeral. The almost incredible summer weather continued as though God was for once on the side of the colliers. Eli Williams, the son of Williams the Road, was reluctant to go to the pit, to put on his dirty, coal-matted, coal-smelling working clothes, stiff and dry, like the dead. He would have preferred to spend the day in the garden, but the night shift officials came off at six and they would be itching to get home. Eli and his two brothers set off, walking through the quiet morning village. No one was out but the cats, windows were blind, doors locked, the striking village was asleep. There was no talking between the brothers. There was nothing to say to a brother. Perhaps sheer quiet was a delight to them after the noise of their kitchen. They walked on together, their heavy boots the only sound under the sun.

In order to reach the colliery office where they reported for work, the three had to pass alongside the Powder House. This was a red brick, green fenced building standing away from the main workings. It housed the explosives. They walked past it, sleepy and morning-eyed, slouching and unwilling. Eli turned his head to see if there were nettles for small beer in the shelter of the building and was suddenly jerked awake and responsive, for the door in the green gate was standing open, the padlock hanging loose, like a grin.

"Oi," he said to his brothers, "look."

They stood stupid for a moment, then Malachi walked through the gate and up to the door.

"This is open too. Broken open it was. We'll have to report this, boys."

"I'll go," Eli shouted and ran, heavy in his boots, his food tin and water bottle lamming at his sides. He went first to the office, but no one was there; too early yet for executives. Then he ran to the lamp-room and found the night shift ready to leave, packing up the cards and the dominoes, for there had not been a great deal of work to do. Eli stood at the door, breathing.

Rees fireman said, "Hullo, what's up with you? Come into money?"

"It's the Powder House. Broken open. Drop dead!"

"W'at the 'ell?"

Rees pushed his way past him, to see for himself. The rest of the night shift straggled after, slow to have it confirmed, wondering whom to blame.

Rees came back into the office. He looked at the telephone, and taking his courage in both hands, while he breathed a prayer, he asked for the number of the Manager's home. Then he put the phone down again as though it could bite. He had remembered that the Manager would not be there. No other official was on the phone. Better send a message to Evan the Under and Sam the clerk. He called two shotsmen from the night shift and sent one to tell the Under-Manager and the other to tell the colliery clerk, that the Powder House had been broken open and gelignite stolen. Would they please come at once?

"You better tell the bobby too," Eli Williams suggested.

"Will you go to Glyndwr Police's then, Eli? And tell him the same!"

"All right. I'll go. Inspector won't half be mad, boy. Who was it, mun?"

"God knows. Jesus Christ, what do it mean? Are they going to blow something up?"

"Don't be daft. Nobody in Cilhendre would blow a cat up."

"Well w'at the 'ell do they want gelignite for then?"

"Somebody found an old drift in the mountain p'raps and wants a bit of coal. There's soft you are, mun, lie on your side a bit. No need to look so white. I don't suppose anybody means harm. And Manager isn't here to eat you, whatever."

"No, thank God for that. Let's hope you're right, boy. But I don't like it, indeed to God."

"I better go. Glyndwr won't like gettin' up with the cockerels, that's a fact. So long."

"So long. And thank you, Eli."

"Nothing boy, nothing. Nice day for a walk."

When Glyndwr Thomas Police heard Eli's story he was frightened. His first fear was that the strikers would blow up the Police Station and him with it, in order to avenge their comrades and the defeat on Thursday night. He buttoned up his uniform coat, drawing comfort from it as a woman does from her corset. The morning sun caught the trail of yesterday's slug. Without his breakfast, he ran to the station and, picking up his old enemy, the telephone, he tossed the baby to the inspector.

Inspector Evans was up early for he had much to do before the Manager's funeral that afternoon. He was shaved and in his best uniform when the telephone bell rang. Fear and trembling came shivering along the lines and blasting and damnation went shuttle-cock back. Mrs. Evans heard in her milk-and-water kitchen and grew smaller, out of sight; Thomas wished he'd had his breakfast for a bit more spunk; the operator, listening in to the call, grinned and loved it.

Inspector Evans shouted for his breakfast, kicked his wife's dog, cursed his porridge and said the tea was cold. He thundered and lightninged out of the house, tripped on his shoe lace, cursed his way to the garage, and climbed into the car. The feel of the steering wheel, firm and black and grooved, soothed his hurts. But the car, like the rest of the world, deserted him; it refused to start. A new storm broke as he swung the starting handle. After four or five cyclonic turns, the engine ticked over and made a promising sound. He leapt to the wheel, but the engine died in an exhausted whisper.

Once more he turned the handle, and, coughing like silicosis, the engine made a better noise. The inspector pretended he was in no hurry, not to tempt Providence, took his time climbing into his seat, and the Rover sang like a siren. He raced through the village to the Police Station, but Thomas had gone home for his breakfast, and all was deserted. The inspector was sorely tried. He drove to Thomas' house and honked the horn continuously until the constable appeared, wiping egg off his chin, and putting on his helmet. Thomas' wife peeped around the lace curtains of her front room, and said "nasty old thing" to the lobster clawed fern in her window.

Not a word was spoken in the car as the policemen drove out to the colliery. The silence shimmered and threatened.

They arrived at the colliery with a great banging of doors and pluming of importance. Rees the fireman, with that bleached look of a well-gnawed bone, was watching for them. He led them to the colliery office where Evan Meredith, the Under-Manager, was waiting. The worry and new responsibility had brought on his indigestion and his handsome face was a bad colour, his eyes dull. He was a man from Cilhendre who had started as a boy underground. All his emotional sympathies were with the colliers, his new social and executive position pulling him awry.

"Well, Meredith, this is a nice kettle of fish. Not making much of a job of things, are you? Mr. Nixon would never have allowed such a thing to happen. It's serious, you know. These strikers will stop at nothing. May blow us all up in our beds before we know where we are."

"Oh, it's not as bad as all that. Just a few sticks of gelignite and a detonator stolen, not enough to blow a building up. There's no need to panic. We've checked the stores and not much is gone. I think that someone has found some old pit workings up in the mountain, there are plenty about and he maybe wants to sell a bit of coal on the q.t."

"Humph. You are far too happy-go-lucky, Meredith. Don't speak too soon. Violent men with explosives. I don't like it. Not at all."

"But this is Cilhendre, man, not Russia."

"It would be Russia if these colliers had half a chance. We need the soldiers here to teach a few of them a lesson. Think what this strike is costing the country, and our Empire. What we need is discipline, a good dose of it. This is the second stage in a campaign, starting with the murder of Mr. Nixon. You mark my words. This is serious, but, thank God, I'm in charge."

"If I didn't have such indigestion, I could talk to you about the strike, but the thought of thinking makes me worse. Let's go to the Powder House." Disgusted and confirmed in his suspicions of Meredith's back-sliding sentiments, the Demon King led the way to The Scene of the Crime.

The strikers were on the tips on Friday morning as usual. The tips had become a social centre for the men. They missed going to work together and they missed the exclusively male friendliness of the pubs. They were not welcomed with empty pockets in the bar and indeed the fear of being thought spongers would have kept most of them away. But the tips were warm and easy and you could make a comfortable seat if you shuffled the slack around and were not too fussy about your clothes. On Friday the talking was about the theft from the Powder House. The night shift officials had brought the news down to their wives and the wives had shaken it out with the breakfast table cloths.

D.J. was picking coal with the others.

"Is it a serious offence, D.J. to steal that gelignite? Would it mean jail?"

"Yes, of course. It's breaking and entering. I don't know what this place is coming to. First the Manager is killed, then we go to jail, and now somebody breaks into the Powder House. Being a magistrate will soon be a full time job."

"Aye, and somebody has a baby on the sly and don't report it. Here's a place! I'll have to move. No class here no more."

"Who'd have you, boyo?"

"God knows. Hell of a thought, isn't it? Nobody wants us colliers."

"They can't do without us, Jim. Don't be so defeated. When the strike has gone on a bit longer, they'll see whether they want us or not. Keep your pecker up, my boy." D.J. tried to speak with the conviction that the men expected from him.

"Who the hell took that gel, mun?"

"I don't think anybody means harm. Perhaps it's for salmon or for an old drift up the mountain."

"Whatever it's for, Jim, it's breaking and entering and a criminal offence. Case for the Assizes it would be."

"Would it? Drop dead."

"Aye, and there'd be a big fuss about it now, with the strike on and men afraid like Griffiths the Owner, not to mention the murder."

"Oi, talk about afraid. Have you heard about Sam the Clerk? When they came to tell him, mun, he was in bed, see, and he came downstairs la-di-dah in a dressing-gown. Red, they say, and white spots. When he heard the Powder House was raided he went green and said he was bad and had to go back to bed. They told him he was wanted at the pit but, no fear, no pit for Sam, he went to bed and I've heard he's caught the nine train to Swansea, bag an' all. Gone away 'till it's safe to come back. No blowin' up for Sam, thank you."

"Who has he got in Swansea, then?"

"His Auntie Rachel lives in Sketty. Safe place, Sketty. No colliers in Sketty."

"Poor bugger. Was he really scared?"

"Aye, took it bad, mun. He thinks we're out for revenge. Been readin' too much."

"Oi, let's give him a real fright. We'll send Threatenin' Letters and sign them with our blood with two sticks of gel for a crest on the top of the paper. Scare his pants off, the daft ha'p'orth. Does he think we're all bolshies or what?"

"The Black Hand in Cilhendre. Where will the Phantom Strike? Is Sam Safe? Oh boy! Come on. Who's got three ha'pence for a stamp?"

"Send it without a stamp and make Sam pay double."

"Stop it now, boys. Play the game. You can't blame the poor devil for being afraid. I'm afraid of plenty."

"Well the silly conk has no business to be afraid of us. Good God, he used to live next door to us in College Row. Wish I knew who had that gel. I'd blackmail him for a stamp for Sam, indeed to God."

"What shall we put in the letter, then?"

"Oh, things from the *Wizard* like 'Vengeance Awaits' and 'We know where you're hid' in red capital letters. There's plenty we can say. You come to our place after soup-kitchen and we'll write it in the parlour."

"Don't indeed, boys." D.J. hated being a spoil-sport.

"You haven't heard any of this, D.J. Go and pick over there, look, there's a nice little cwtch by there."

"It's you'll be in jail next, my lad, not me. I'll be on the Bench to send you there, for writing menacing letters. Like it says in the *Wizard*, 'You have been warned.'"

"Davy! You don't say!"

"I do say. Sam might turn nasty and take the letters to Swansea police and then where would I be?"

"On the Bench, boy. We'd have plenty of free grub in jail."

"Didn't you have enough jail on Wednesday night?"

"They weren't bad chaps, those bobbies. Fair play. Like the All Whites, they're a bit better on their home ground."

"Garn! There's a team. Pack of bloody old women."

"You think you're the damn Selection Committee since you been to Twickenham once, don't you? Be playin' for Wales next, not 'arf. You're only jealous because you wasn't in jail."

"They say young Ike Isaac is shaping up for a nice little forward. Be fine to have a cap in Cilhendre, wouldn't it? Wait till he puts a bit more weight on and I think he'll be worth his place."

"How's he going to put on weight? On the Parish? If anybody puts on weight in Cilhendre we ought to boycott him for a blackleg. Anybody going to the funeral?"

"No. Private it is. Relatives only."

"Funny sort of funeral. I don't think I'd be much for that. I likes a good big funeral with plenty of singing and gallons of crying."

"Who'll sing in Manager's, then?"

"I don't suppose they'll have much singing."

"No singing in a funeral? Damn, I'd die if I couldn't have singing in my funeral."

"Dope, you'd be dead already."

"Well, I'd haunt them then. You can't have a funeral without hymns – be like drowning the cat, mun."

"Wonder if she'll cry. The girls there say she hasn't lost a tear over him. Can't say I blame her, but it would look better, wouldn't it? Tidier, somehow – unless she bumped him off, of course."

"There'll be plenty of crying tomorrow, whatever, in Gwen's funeral. Poor kid, young to go, too."

"Aye. Not much of a life was it?"

"Gerwin is taking it awful bad, isn't he, Davy?"

"Yes, indeed, Gerwin is beside himself. We can't do any-thing with him. He's in a very bad way."

"There we are again, see," the revolutionary of the police cell spoke up, "that girl has been murdered by economic conditions; if she had had proper nourishment as a kid, she wouldn't have caught the old germ. And if she'd had any money she could have gone to Switzerland to be cured, instead of being sent home incurable from the old Sanatorium. You wait till we have a Revolution or they nationalise the pits, any one will do, we'll all claim a decent wage – the money we deserve and our kids won't die of T.B. no more. We'll have good food and good houses and, boys, we'll have work; guaranteed, regular work. Sounds too good, don't it?"

"What do you think nationalisation is? Magic? You can't nationalise germs and doctors, mun."

"No, but if you get plenty of food and good houses, you are helping the doctors to fight the old germs."

"Is he sayin' right, D.J.?"

"Yes, of course it's right. Why do you think the T.B. figures are so high here and in Ireland? Because we are poor, boy, poor in a world of plenty. I think nationalisation is the answer to our problem here, but we are not the only hungry ones, God knows. When I think of the amount of hunger there is in this world, my belly shrinks inside me. And I shrink with it. We are all so small and useless. What the hell's the good of committees?" and he picked up the largest piece of slag as he spoke. He threw it away from him, he finished speaking and it landed with a silly ineffectual plop in the soft slack. "See?" he said.

"Why don't you read Karl Marx, then, D.J.? He's got all the answers."

"I have read him, boy, but if you can make sense out of 'Capital' you're a better man than I took you for. A man called Aveling has written a simple account of what Marx said, but even that is as clear as mud sometimes. And I don't agree with all I've understood either. One thing he said is that the workers will continue to get steadily worse off. Now that isn't true for a start. We don't take the women and children underground now, and they used to less than a hundred years ago. Then there's that about religion, the opium of the masses, I don't agree with him there. Have you read that book by Upton Sinclair called *The Jungle?* It's about Chicago and their troubles there. I've got it if you'd like to borrow it. It breaks your heart, honest. Oh, the poor, the poor, God help us."

"Does God help us, or think of us, Davy?"

"Well, he helps me, whatever. Speak for yourself, but I know that I do feel better after I've prayed. But I believe in God. And you can mutter opium as much as you like, Jim Fullpelt."

"Well I go to chapel, but I don't know what I believe in. I only go for the singin'."

"Aye, there's a tidy few singers in Bethel, all right. But I haven't got a Sunday suit no more, worse luck."

"Has Gerwin's brother come from Slough yet, D.J.?"

"He's coming tonight we hope. I'll be glad to see him, perhaps he'll be a bit of help to old Gerwin."

"Aye, Iorwerth is a steady boy. He did the right thing, getting away from the valleys while he could. But he must be awful homesick. I'd never have the guts to leave, even if I had the fare. No mountains nor singing in Slough, and everybody talking English all the time. No thanks, I think I'd rather starve by here now."

"Aye it would be hard to leave, but you got to eat. Can't eat hymns."

"And you got to have fire to cook a bit of food, my mussus won't half tamp when she sees the spoonful I've got in this sack. Come winter, it'll be hard."

"We'll be back before winter, you'll see. Come you, they'll be beggin' us on their knees for coal before winter. We'll win in the end, never you fear."

"Let's hope, whatever. I owes the Parish so much, I'll have to live to a hundred to pay it back. And what we owes the Co-op is nobody's business."

"We'll have big money after this, mun. You'll be able to give the Parish a bloody cheque. Paid with thanks, James Jones."

"There's the hooter. Let's go. Seven course dinner at Cilhendre soup kitchen. Roll up boys, rush the gates."

"Look, don't forget, don't write that letter to Sam. We've got enough trouble in Cilhendre; use your heads now."

"All right, D.J., have it your own way again; I don't think we got a envelope, anyway."

"Dinner is served, gentlemen. Come on, what are we waitin' for?"

At the inquest on Friday the police offered formal evidence of identity and asked for an adjournment.

Luncheon at Mrs. Nixon's house was a cold business of ill-assorted relatives. Mr. Nixon's sister, Mrs. Powell, was the only representative of his family. She was fat and normally cosy, but today she was so overawed by her thin sister-in-law that she hardly breathed for nerves, among the silver and mahogany and table mats. She had quarrelled with her brother and had not spoken to him for many years, but, remembering her mother and her own youth; she was moved and sentimental. She had cried when she arrived at the house that morning, but her sister-in-law had looked so surprised down her nose that Mrs. Powell felt tears must be very bad manners. She wore a black coat over a black dress of an ageless style that had never known fashion, but she was proud of the "bit of good" on her coat collar and of

her gold brooch that said "Mother". Her rather abstracted
manner was due in part to nervousness and in part to her
concentration on remembering everything in the house, so
that she would have a great deal to tell when she got home
to Pant.

The other guests were the prosperous Dowalls. Three thin
men, with big bones in their faces and big bony hands. Two
were Mrs. Nixon's brothers, the third an uncle. One of the
brothers had brought his wife. She too was fat, but never
cosy. So corseted was she and firm that she felt to the touch
like a dead crusader on his tomb. Her hair was tinted fair and
the pearls she wore were real. When John looked at his aunts
he could not but think of the social significance of corseting.
How far had the discipline of the corset affected the course
of human affairs, he wondered. Corset all working-class
women and . . . He pulled up his thoughts and concentrated
on looking after the guests.

Conversation at luncheon was difficult. Every subject
offered its pitfall. The murder and inquests were obviously
ruled out; the strike was tabooed because Mrs. Powell's
husband was himself on strike and Mrs. Powell had already
indicated, nerves notwithstanding, that her views on the
subject were both fixed and strong. The political situation
was too much like the strike for comfort. Gardens were a
great standby, of course. Gardens and the flora and fauna
of Cilhendre sustained them for most of the meal. Mrs. Powell
upset the equilibrium somewhat when she described the
garden of their minister at Pant who unfortunately bore the
name of Jeffries. And quite suddenly, it seemed, it was time
for the funeral service.

When they left the familiar things of the dining-room John
felt wrapped up in a thick blanket of unreality. The maids
had set the stage during the meal and the conversation. Now
the curtain was going up, the house was hushed and darkened, the flowers looked as waxen and artificial as the body

and the coffin, the actors vaguely hovered in the wings, wondering whether there wouldn't be time to make a quick trip upstairs. John was suddenly sure that none of them had ever been alive. He was the male lead and did not know his lines. The unreality was almost palpable. His mother was wearing a mask of control, the uncles impossibly tall and thin and serious. Where was the garden, the flora and fauna? The kindly vicar came up and took John by the hand, but not even his so living presence could make the words of the service in the drawing-room anything but incongruous, false, cold and terrifying. The boy ached to escape the intoxicating flowers, the mesmerising words, the hypnotic coffin. He looked towards the door for sanctuary, and saw that the two maids were sitting near it, crying quietly into their handkerchiefs. "What's Hecuba to him or he to Hecuba?" The shock of seeing them and the relief of muttering a suitable quotation restored him in a small measure. Suddenly the service was over. Time seemed to be jerking forward like a train when it first starts to leave a station. John felt no continuity, he was pulled puppetwise from one impossible situation to another. The coffin, the flowers, his top hat, his gloves and John stepped into the first car. His great uncle followed him in and banged the door like a full stop but the sentence went on. The two Dowall brothers followed in the second car and Inspector Evans, the manager's friend, came in a third. Blinds were drawn in all the houses along the road and men in the street stood bareheaded and sorry, to watch them pass.

The three women remained in the house, embarrassed, polite, relieved and flat. The two girls had watched the cars move off through rainbows of tears and had gone back to the kitchen to blow their noses and put their hankies away.

"Oh, there's a funeral. I wouldn't bury a dog like it. Nobody was even cryin' but us."

"Why were you crying, Liz?"

"I always cry in funerals. I think of our Mam. I keep thinking it's Mam in the old coffin and it all comes back to me. Why was you crying then?"

"I don' know. Breakin' my heart I was, and I haven't got anybody dead. There's soft, isn't it?"

"Oh, I don' know if it's soft. Pity for him too. I wonder if they'll ever find out. Some say it's Elwyn Jeffries Jess, for sure. They'll hang him if it is."

"What sort of funeral do they get if they're hanged, Liz?"

"Oh, it's 'orrible. They have the funeral first when the man is still alive. He has to listen, and then they bury him quiet in quick-lime and that eats him all up and in no time there's nothing left. No relatives come nor nothing. By himself he is, with all them strangers."

"No. Honest?"

"Yes, they do, then."

"Fancy hearing all that about ashes to ashes about yourself and waiting for it. No. I don't believe it. Nobody could. I don't think they really hang them at all. They keep them locked up out of sight just, and pretend they are dead, to frighten people."

"Go on. It's true. They put a notice up outside the jail and a doctor signs it to say the man is dead good and proper. It's no good saying it's too horrible – it's true, I tell you. It's no good being like that woman from Pontardulais who saw a giraffe and said, 'I won't believe it.'"

"Well, shut up about it now then. Makes me feel sick. I won't sleep all night. Let's talk about something else. Are you going to the dance Saturday?"

CHAPTER 14

A prayer meeting was held in Bethel on Friday evenings. As D. J. Williams walked towards the chapel, he met Inspector Evans. The inspector walked subdued, like a man who has been to a funeral.

"Things are in a bad way here, Mr. Williams."

"Yes, indeed. You haven't found the culprits then?"

"No, not yet. It's been a trying day, I can tell you. I've been on the phone to the Chief and he is very disturbed. Those were his words, very disturbed."

"Yes, I'm sure he must be. You went to the funeral, no doubt?"

"I managed that, yes."

"How are the family? Is the old trouble much on their minds?"

"I suppose it is. But to tell the truth, it's hard to tell what's on her mind. I didn't stay to talk this afternoon. I'm busy. I want this gelignite business cleared up. But we haven't got far yet. We found a cap up near the Powder House and I thought we had got the culprit for sure, but we can't find out who it belongs to. This is the second cap we've found, now. There's one good thing, awful careless criminals you produce in Cilhendre. This cap now, was one of two dozen that came in to Morgans Drapers months ago – all alike brown and white checks – and of course, Morgans doesn't remember who bought them."

"If he had two dozen I should think he wouldn't remember. There's no distinguishing mark on it?"

"No, nothing, nothing but a smell of fish if you please. The smell of fish and a bit of fern caught under the peak."

"No other clues?"

"No. The padlocks were filed off and the lock of the door cut out with a saw."

"Must be somebody with tools then. But no, most people have a file and saw, don't they? Smelling of fish too, that's funny. Fish in a cap."

"I'm going up to the pit again before it gets dark. I'm feeling quite depressed, Mr. Williams, and no mistake. If only Mr. Nixon was here, I used to be able to talk to him about things. I'll miss him."

"Yes, I'm sorry, Mr. Evans, indeed. It's hard to lose a friend. I won't keep you now, then, I'm going to chapel myself."

"So long, then. I'm going to fetch the car. It's a long walk."

"Goodnight."

D.J. walked on towards the doors of Bethel. He muttered "fish in a cap". Who'd carry fish in a cap? He went to his seat in the big bilious chapel, pea green walls, yellow varnished pitch pine, frieze and organ pipes "picked out" with pink and gold-leaf. He bent his head to ask a blessing and having tucked his hat safely under the seat under cover of the prayer, he looked around to see who was in the chapel. Only a fistful of people came to the weekday meetings, the deacons, the caretaker, the deputy organist. The oldest deacon came in after D.J., followed by the young niece who kept house for him. Three women came in together. There was quiet in the chapel, but a comfortable quiet without the pomp and dressing of Sunday. One of the three women passed peppermints to her companions with a great show of secrecy. The oldest deacon stood up and announced that they would begin with "Abide with me". The singing was poor and sporadic and full of flat notes and smelt of peppermints. Then the old man prayed to the Lord in whom we live and move and have our being; it was his recognised opening gambit and no one else in Bethel would have borrowed it for the world. He prayed for the two stricken families in the village and for mercy upon those two souls who had been taken from their midst to face the Almighty Throne of Grace. When his prayer was over he changed gear into his talking voice and asked the woman of the peppermints to suggest a hymn.

The hymn she chose was "Bringing in the Sheaves", rather prematurely, perhaps. The tune was very hard on the few sopranos. It had been a relief to her that he had not asked her to pray, for one of her great and terrifying nightmares was that one day she would be driven by some inner compulsion to stand up in the chapel and give in public a catalogue of all her debts and then go on to tell the deacons what she thought they were like in bed. This fear would awaken her at night and leave her with nerves jangled and hands sweaty. It was only slightly better than her other dream – that all her children were running out into the road and under the wheels of the inspector's car.

During the meeting D.J. could not concentrate on the service, though half of his mind gathered the sheaves with vigour. But he kept repeating "fish in a cap" to himself. He imagined a cutlet of hake sitting neatly in the middle of a cloth cap. Then he thought, hake wasn't the only fish, in spite of the chip shops. What about salmon, now – salmon – Elwyn Jeffries and Cray Reservoir – no, no, there are other fish too, and salmon was much too big for a cap. There was trout now, and he remembered Gerwin catching three small speckled trout and wrapping them in ferns to take home to Gwen on Thursday morning.

The stupid service would never end. He had heard all the prayers before. God, make them finish their praying, he prayed, I want to go home. Let us get outside where we can think honestly. Fish in a cap, trout wrapped up in ferns, Gerwin. Gerwin burying the baby. Gerwin with trout in his cap. God let them finish. God let me get out.

After the service D.J. said a brisk Good Night and walked quickly away from the chapel. This was almost blasphemy for the slow funeral walk down the chapel steps with a word or two about the meeting is as much part of religious rites as taking off the hat in the front porch. The deacons were disappointed, they liked a word with Davy.

The magistrate thought that perhaps he ought to go to the police station at once with his suspicions but remembered with a gulp of relief that the inspector was up at the colliery. Better go home and ask Gerwin. Gerwin would tell him the truth and there might well be nothing in his fears at all. Going home would at least give him time to think out what to do.

Meanwhile, the inspector had walked to the police station to collect a car and a constable. He drove up to the pit with Thomas at his side. Glyndwr Thomas was still as nervous as a mosquito and sat as far as possible into the corner of the seat. But the inspector was full of the mystique of the funeral and suitably quiet.

The officials on duty at Cilhendre Colliery were now the afternoon shift, and were as alert as geese for trespassers. A policeman guarded the door to the Powder House. The sound of the Rover brought the afternoon shift together like an accident.

"Nothing to report, Inspector," said the Overman.

"Right. Now will you do something for me? The constables and I have been over as much of this ground as we can manage, but there's not enough of us. I want you to set any of your men that you can spare to comb all the approaches to the pit. Go over every path and all the sidings to see if you can find anything at all that looks like a clue. Beat down the grass and the nettles. He left his cap behind him, and he may have dropped something else in his hurry. Follow the paths right to the end, into the village, or up the station or even to the farms. Don't give up."

"We comes off at ten, sir."

"Well, it isn't eight yet. You've got a good two hours. Come on now, show a bit of spirit. Let's get this thing tidy before the inquest is resumed. Think about me for a change – I don't go off at ten tonight or any night. Noses to the grindstone, boys, and quick march. Get it done before dark, there's good boys, or we may wake to find ourselves blown up."

The men looked at each other, felt a bit soft, but decided to be helpful. They found bits of sticks about and, armed like Boy Scouts, they set off in couples to play detective.

"There's one good thing about this strike, Thomas, none of our suspects can run away before tomorrow. Nobody's got any money and they wouldn't get far on foot."

"No, that's right enough. Not unless they steal your car," Thomas said, with a flash of hope in his eyes.

"Talk sense will you?"

"They might blow it up perhaps," Thomas continued yearningly. "You better drain all the petrol out or there'll be a fire."

Such sacrilege was enough to bring the Inspector back from the fields of Christian sentimentality where he had browsed since the funeral. The bull was back in his pen, head down to all corners. He stamped and bellowed his evening away until the searchers began to come back from their tracking.

The first find was fresh orange peel, rare enough of late to qualify as an oddity at least, the second a rotten rusted old working boot, then a cancelled return bus ticket to Swansea, an empty Woodbine packet. The men with the real clue came slowly and unwilling to the office, reluctant and guilty over their find. It was a file with the initials G.E. burned in the handle. The shotsman who carried it laid it gently on the office table, beside the orange peel and the bus ticket. He took his hand away slowly as if he would pull the thing back again. The Inspector's hands shook as he lunged for it, like a man in a sexual passion, even his breath came heavy.

"A clue," he said, as he might have said "the Holy Grail" with reverential awe. "G.E. Who is G.E.?"

"Christ," said Thomas.

The colliery officials looked at each other and looked away.

"It can't be. It may not be anyone from Cilhendre at all. It hasn't got to be him."

"Who? Who?" The bull was tossing his horns.

"He may have lent it to somebody."

"Perhaps he lost it and somebody else found it."

"It may have been dropped weeks ago. There hasn't been much rain."

"Damn you. Who is it? Who is G.E.? Thomas, who is G.E.?"

"Well the only G.E. I call think of in Cilhendre is Gerwin. Gerwin Evans. But it can't be him, not with Gwen —"

"No, not Gerwin. He must have lent it I tell you. There's no harm in Gerwin, he's a good boy."

"Of course he is."

"Well, then he must give us an explanation. We'll hear what he has to say. There is no doubt at all that file has been used very recently. Look, there are still grains of steel in the teeth. We'll go and ask him."

"You can't, sir. Indeed to God you can't. The funeral is tomorrow and they say he's taking it awful bad."

"Funeral or not, I'm taking no risks. I'll have to ask him what he knows. As you say, somebody may have borrowed his file, or it may not be his at all. If so, he is the best person to ask. Come, come, the matter is far too serious for any sort of soft feelings. Thomas, come with me in the car. Where does he live?"

"Next door to D. J. Williams, they're big buddies. But I don't like to go, drop dead."

"Well, thank you, men. You have been a very great help to me. Come along, Thomas, come along."

The car was driven off and the men on the pit head looked crushed and small and quiet, brought face to face with the meaning and the horror of the law.

CHAPTER 15

When D.J. got to his home he saw Gerwin standing in the garden, near the hedge which separated the two gardens. Gerwin was tearing bits of green out of the privet as he had done that other afternoon. He stood tall and gaunt against the setting sun, like a poster picture of all miners, all workers, it was too realistic to be true. He was watching for Davy.

"I'd like to speak to you for a minute, Davy, if you don't mind." He looked ageless, like a symbol from John Donne, like a nightmare, like a sick man.

"Yes, Gerwin, I wanted to see you too. Come in, will you?"

They went into Ann Williams' kitchen, empty but for Brit.

"Sit down, Gerwin, there's something I want to ask you."

"No, I don't want to sit. You sit. I'll stand by here and look out of the window. It's nice by the window and I like to see the sun."

"All right, boy, all right." D.J. suddenly realised that he was humouring Gerwin, giving him his way as he might to a child and he felt cold with a weight of fear. He refused his thoughts. He did not ask his own questions. "What is it, Ger, what did you want to see me about?"

"Davy, remember us talking that time in Neath and me asking you about the Catholics, don't you? You do remember. Say you remember."

"Yes, yes. Of course."

"You said the preacher was like a kind of father to them, didn't you? You said he loved them all the same and he was their friend and helped them when they did wrong. You're sure you remember? You said about confessing – didn't you? Davy, boy, you are not a preacher, thank God, but you have

147

always been a friend to me. We started school the same day and when they laughed at my funny hair you helped to fight them. You must be my friend now, Davy. Say you'll be my friend or I might hurt you, perhaps. Don't let me down, Davy. I got to talk, see. You let me tell you. I got to talk, I got to tell. No. Don't you say nothing now. You said if they confessed part of the burden was gone, you said it showed their faith in the Mercy. I have got faith, Davy, and I got to tell you. I got to lift the burden a bit. You told me all about it in Neath. Listen now. Don't say nothing. Listen. Tell God to forgive me Davy, you forgive me too. You tell God, you're better than me. Help me Davy, help."

"Gerwin, I'm here, boy, I'm with you."

"Gwen it was. She had a little baby, only don't say. It was a lovely baby and we was going to ask my sister-in-law in Slough, our Janet, to say it was hers. We didn't want anybody to know. But it died, see, Davy. It was all for nothing. She suffered. I never thought – "in pain thou shalt bring forth", but we don't know about the pain, it was like the burning fire, it was scorching and withering. And the baby was dead. I made the coffin. And she was listening. She heard every blow of the hammer, nails in her coffin too. She knew, she counted the nails. Doing sums she was, and her poor mind wandering, saying tables, twice two is four. It was my fault, Davy. She was listening to the hammer. The hammering killed her, up and down, up and down."

"But she was very ill already, Ger!"

"Aye, but the hammer finished her and I did it, see. That night I promised to bury the little one. Dewi we called him. She wanted it in the churchyard, in a little corner for nobody to notice and I promised. But I didn't manage it, see. I broke my promise, but I said the prayers. I said them quick and perhaps wrong. But I said them. I did say them. "Our Father" and I sang a hymn quiet with my cap off. But not in the churchyard. I didn't keep my word. I broke my promise. Gwen, can you hear me Gwen? I tried, honest I tried. The sun's going down, look Davy, see how red the sky is? Shepherds' delight."

"Yes, boy, yes."

"Are you there Davy? Are you sitting there?"

"Yes, come you."

"I promised it would be in the churchyard, but I couldn't wait very late, see, I don't like the churchyard after dark. Digging after twelve, no never. I don't like it after twelve. It's like underground when you feel all of a sudden that your butties have gone, that there's nobody near but you and the rats. But there's worse than rats in that old churchyard. They would be there with me, watching me, all my sins on my back and they there lying dead in wait. I didn't wait long enough, it should have been later. There I was carrying the coffin by the bridge and he came to me. I thought it was Satan, I thought the devil himself had come to meet me, but then I saw his fancy trousers. He spoke to me, Davy, laid hands on the little one's bed and it fell and opened. He was staring there, all lighted up he looked and he said bad things. Things about Gwen and about the strike and you. He said he'd tell everybody about Gwen, and tell the polices unless I went back to work and blacklegged. He called Gwen names, bad names. It was my fault, I told him when he saw the baby that it was Gwen's little one. Then he called her names and I hit him. I hit him and he fell down. He was an old nuisance. He wasted my time. I thought to leave him by the road but somebody might see, so I dragged him under the bridge, out of the way. Good job too because somebody passed, up to the mountain. I heard and I hid. I must have dropped him in a puddle. Serve him right, he should mind his tongue. I'll give him tongue. I'm sorry Davy, look I've pulled your mother's curtain. It's torn. Sorry, Davy. What was I saying? Was I telling you the confessing part?"

"Yes, Ger. About hiding by the bridge."

"Yes, yes. I hid and they went up the mountain. Laughing, they were. Not right to laugh in a funeral is it? They went up the mountain and they went. But it was too late. Nearly twelve by then so I dug the grave where I was, by there, by the river. I thought if I said the prayers that would make it all right. Do you think he'll go to Heaven, Davy, with only prayers and me and no holy ground?"

"Yes, yes, of course, don't worry about that; that part is right, for sure. Suffer little children."

"Thank you, Davy, thank you. This confessing is nice Davy. Lovely. Like swimming in deep water with no old clothes, like up the mountain when we was boys. Now let me finish now. I never knew before it was nice to talk. I haven't been much of a talker. More of a listener I was, not like you. I said the prayers and I whispered the hymn and I sprinkled the earth and covered him up. I was afraid too, Davy. I was thinking the Devil would rise up from where I'd hidden him. Satan was hiding by the bridge, waiting for me to pass again, but when I went to make sure and not be afraid, he had changed to Manager again. I think he was dead. What do Catholics do after the confessing, Davy?"

"Oh, Gerwin, boy, I don't know. I don't know any more what anybody does."

"P'raps they pray. Will you pray with me? Pray something about forgiveness; Jesus and the blood of the lamb and the mercy and the glory. I didn't like the blood, but the confessing part is finished now. Go on, Davy, pray now, there's a good boy. We used to play preachers. You was a fine preacher then. Pray now on your knees here by the window by me."

But Davy was already praying for guidance, for a bit of wisdom and the energy to carry it through.

"Say it loud, Davy, for me to hear."

"Our Father, look upon us, two sinners. Help us to see what we must do."

"Yes, Amen. Go on."

"Guide us in Thy infinite wisdom to do what Thou would have us do. Thy way, not mine, O Lord, however dark it be. Be Thou my light, my guide, my wisdom and my all."

Davy's voice was breaking and faltering but Gerwin's hand was firm and strong upon his shoulder.

"Just a little bit more."

D.J. could not think up prayers. He recited hymns:

> "Oh brother man, fold to thy heart thy brother,
>   Where pity dwells the peace of God is there.
>   To worship rightly is to love each other,
>   Each smile a hymn, each kindly deed a prayer."

The hand pressed on his shoulder again.

> "Lead kindly light, amid the encircling gloom,
>   Lead Thou me on;
>   The night is dark, and I am far from home,
>   Lead Thou me on."

"Amen, and may the peace of God go with the two of us," added the murderer. "Thank you very much, Davy. I'll go now. P'raps take a walk and meet Iorwerth off the train. See you tomorrow. So long." He spoke casually, as though he had just been in to borrow matches.

Davy was alone. Defeated, bewildered, man in a whirlpool. A good man who no longer knew by instinct what was right and what was wrong. A man who had been good because the good had always been the simple, natural, compelling way. He had never before been faced with this sort of moral conflict. He had prayed himself dry and had no one to turn to. Right and wrong should be clear cut like black and white; if only Christianity was a bit more logical; but that would be the end of it. Murder was black sin, that was no problem, but confession? – then treachery was a sin too. He was not a priest, he was a magistrate. But he was a friend too, he had been trusted. But Gerwin was ill, his mind was failing – he might do more harm. Well, I can't hold him down. He's stronger than me. The police could. Then I'll have to tell them. Tell them about poor Gwen, was that loyalty? – the good is oft interred with their bones. Gwen, she hardly seems to have lived a minute, she used to look so pretty going to school. The Inspector is up at the pit now. Well, it's too far to walk. I'm too tired. I wonder if he's found anything out. But what about that gelignite? I forgot to ask him after all. Has he got it? Tired or not I'll have to go and find out.

D.J. drove himself next door. His hands were shaking, he crammed his hat on his head and leaned against the door jamb, to breathe and count up to ten, slowly.

"Is Gerwin in, Mrs. Evans?"

"No. He came in for a minute just now to say he was going for a little walk up the mountain. He seemed a bit better after your little chat, better than he's been since . . . all the week."

"All right, then. I'll look in later, he may be back then, and Iorwerth too. Mam is with you, isn't she?"

"Yes, she's here. We'll be all right."

"So long, now."

A kind of cold had seized D.J. The goose-flesh ran up his arms and he felt a premonition of some further disaster which he could not name. He must find Gerwin. He knew he had to find him but he couldn't do it alone. He must find someone to come with him. Up the mountain. Where would he go on the mountain? The Big Rock, of course. He used to sit there often to watch the birds and look down over Cilhendre. We used to play there when we were children, the rock was a throne, a castle, a fort, a little house. He was always faithful to it. But the way up is steep and treacherous, what about this old chest. Who'll come with me? Elwyn will. Yes, Elwyn.

D.J. hurried and stumbled to Elwyn Jeffries' house. It was a sad house, crushed under the threat of the impending inquest. Jess had given up her struggle and was breaking her heart into a white dish towel with "glass" written on it in blue. The children were in bed, dreaming horrors, and Elwyn was doggedly concentrating on a walking stick he was carving for himself out of a holly branch. D.J. was beyond finesse.

"Elwyn, come with me, will you? I want your help. Don't worry, Jess. It'll be all right. Just believe me now. Don't worry any more. Go to bed and sleep, there's a good girl. But let Elwyn come with me."

Elwyn stood and stretched his fair height and Jess went on her knees to tidy away the chips of wood from his carving. She looked up at D.J., her poor face red and swollen and drowned. He touched her shoulder and nodded his head and turned away to the door. While Elwyn reached for his cap and tied his collier's muffler, D.J. told him he was concerned about Gerwin who was out on the mountain and depressed. He did not say why he was worried, he couldn't rationalise his fears and they were all the more powerful for that.

"We'll ask Everynight to come with us, Davy. He knows all the short cuts and I sometimes think he can see in the dark. The moon won't be up yet awhile and it'll be dark soon. Come August, comes night."

"All right, but hurry will you?"

"Yes, I'll run on and fetch him, it's only a step and he's in tonight I know, worrying, like me. He's gone and given me an alibi and it won't work, the silly conk."

The three hurrying men beat along the canal bank in the darkening evening. The still, stagnant water held the last of the day's light, willows grew on the far side, throwing deep, shadows over the tins and broken buckets, boots and a bicycle frame in the water. At the lock gates, closed beyond memory, floated the flotsam of carnival – bright papers, tinsel, chocolate wrappers, an apple core. D.J. had to lean on the rusty iron mechanism to catch his breath and Everynight spat at a questing water rat. The rat scuttled away into the willow roots and the three hurried on again. They crossed a plank bridge to leave the canal and turned right to start the mountain climb.

"Why do you think he'd go to the Big Rock, D.J.?"

"I feel it, Joe, that's all. He always liked that place. When he'd had a hiding as a kid he'd always go there after, and we used to play up there, he and I, more than any of you kids down the bottom end of Cilhendre. He felt it was his bit of private property in a way, the old land-owner, God help."

"Are you afraid he'd do himself some harm, like?"

"I don't know. I don't like it. He shouldn't be by himself, whatever."

"No, he's been very funny lately. Very odd he's been."

"Look, boys, I think he took the gelignite."

"Good God! did 'e? What the 'ell would he want it for?"

The same fear was bitten back in their minds. All three were miners who knew the dangers and ways of gelignite.

The path they followed grew steep and the going hard. It was a sheep track and the grass was springy and slippery. Tufty hummocks of coarse grass grew on either side and on the right was a patch of burnt gorse skeletons. In the distance there was a fire where a farmer had set the bracken alight. For D.J. it was a picture of desolation. They walked in single file, hardly speaking, Joe leading them the shortest way to the Big Rock. The light was leaving the sky to the starlings. Joe plunged into a little copse of alders and birches where, earlier, the children had gathered wood anemones. Blackberry flowers pearled in the dusk among brambles, and the men passed on.

"We'll see the rock against the sky when we get through the wood, but it'll be a steep drag up, Davy."

"I know, never mind. I'll manage. Strength according to the need, boy."

They crossed a small peaty drain where the ground was boggy and sucked their boots. It was almost dark in the wood. There was no sight or sound of Gerwin.

The policemen were also making their way up the mountain. They had found from Gerwin's mother that he was out for a walk on the mountain, that he had needed some air and was probably at his favourite place, the Big Rock. Inspector Evans would brook no delay, beginning once more to believe that Gerwin, as "one of these strikers", purposed to blow something up. He was always enthusiastic over his strong, if short-lived, convictions. The two policemen trudged up the mountain-side along a different route from D.J.'s. Their's was the longer way, along the orthodox paths, but they had a start on the other party, for D.J. was a slow walker and had spent some time collecting his friends.

The two groups were approaching the rock from different directions. It was now almost completely dark. The inspector was regretting his impetuosity in climbing this mountain, but he was never a man to show any weakness of purpose and goaded himself onwards by blustering and shouting at his constable. D.J. and his companions heard these familiar sounds from afar and were encouraged in the belief that Gerwin was not after all alone.

They reached the edge of the wood and saw the Big Rock silhouetted before them, dark and blue above their heads. They paused to look up, and called. As they looked for an answer they saw a small flickering light on the blue rock.

"He's got a candle up there. He's made himself at home,

whatever. Hoi, Gerwin, are you there, boy." Everynight's voice rang loud and confident.

The inspector gave an answering shout from where he was bossing up the slope. The sounds of other voices eased the tensions in both groups. The night lost its mystery and its threat. It became a night like other nights. The men came off the stage and were chaps from Cilhendre again. D.J. was abandoned by his demons, he felt he had come back into the light from some terrible nightmare, he murmured "ex tenebris" to himself. The inspector called out to the others, asking who they were and whether Gerwin was with them. As his question hung unanswered between them, a thunder shook the ground, light blinded their darkened eyes, the Big Rock split like a pea-pod and a fearful shadow gibbered for a moment on the open ground at the foot of the rock. A shadow of a man who staggered, seemed to disintegrate and then to vanish in a cloud of sound and rock and flame.

The miners instinctively threw themselves to the ground and Davy rocketed blessedly unconscious. Bits of rock and trees, clothing and flesh and earth rained down around them. Slowly the echoes ceased, the last bit of debris bounced to stillness and the newly risen moon threw a thin light to the crouching men.

CHAPTER 16

The sun came back to Cilhendre on Saturday morning. The people woke and were hungry, ate breakfast and were hungry and looked forward to the soup kitchen. They were ashamed that they could eat but, having eaten and accepted their inhumanity, they accepted all that had happened. It was all true, it was history, it would be in the papers; after that they could be hungry and go up to the garden without feeling slightly guilty. With children and dogs about, it was hard to maintain a sense of unreality, even though the Chief Constable was in Cilhendre. The black clothes had to be sorted and brushed for the funeral, for even the funeral went on.

The adjourned inquests were held that afternoon. D.J. told the story of Gerwin's confession to him. He told only one lie – that he did not know the mother of the child that Gerwin had buried on Tuesday night. It was a child that Gerwin had fathered, he said, and had buried quietly to keep the scandal from being spread. Gerwin's brother, fresh from Slough, had handed the inspector a crumpled untidy note that Gerwin had left for him. "Dear Iorwerth, Look after Mam. Tell the police I done it to the Manager. Sorry. Your loving brother, Gerwin Evans."

The inspector was only half satisfied, of course. He was muttering imprecations and meaningless clichés about cheating the hangman, defeating justice, breaking the law, as though he, representing the law, had more claim to poor Gerwin's poor body than the man had had himself. As though in some obscure, obscene way, a bloodless institution, a man-framed body of Government decrees, a tangle of codes and codicils, had become an entity with claims and a will of its own.

Jess Jeffries was not called to give evidence. It was decided by the police to let sleeping dogs lie, as the inspector profoundly expressed it. They brought a verdict of murder, against Gerwin and suicide while of unsound mind.

Gwen's funeral that afternoon was one of the largest remembered in Cilhendre. The numbers were swollen by the morbidly curious, but most of those present went to show their deep feeling for the mother, a little, punch-drunk, yellow widow. Mrs. Nixon sent a wreath, Elwyn Jeffries sent a salmon to help feed the visiting relatives, Everynight brought his five shillings fox money because he claimed that Maggie's beer was flat that week, and Maggie herself sent down a dozen bottles of stout so that Mrs. Evans could keep up her strength. The emotion and the crying at that funeral would have more than satisfied Liz and Rita Manager. The little baby was buried too, after his inquest, his moment. A short formal service for the unbaptised, with policemen for pallbearers, and no flowers, no tears, no hymns. But the ground was consecrated, all was well.

It was a sadly moving day for Cilhendre. But, somehow, satisfying. Emotions were released and relaxed by the sublimity of Christian burial. For Gwen they could believe in it all. John Nixon, representing his family at the service, felt that what had been mumbo-jumbo for his father was for Gwen the necessary truth, and was furious with his own illogicality. He was moved almost beyond bearing.

The congregation was uplifted by the service and the singing. Some inner need was satisfied, the opium of the poor was a powerful drug, and they left the chapel feeling refreshed and belonging and reassured for the time.

There was a note of anti-climax. There had to be. Jack Look-Out and Tommy had been to the service and as they turned up Mafeking Terrace in their black ties and brown shoes, well brushed suits and bowler hats, Sarah Look-Out was standing on her doorstep waiting for Jack. There was murder in her ferret face. She was holding a broom under her arm, leaning on it, as on a crutch.

"So you've come back, you old devil. Don't think I 'aven't found out. Don't you dare come in by here. I'm packin' your bags and you can go. I'll live on the Parish. I'll starve. I'll go on the streets of Swansea before I let you come back you old devil. I'll give you my father's bit of china. My poor father in his grave, quiet and doin' no harm to nobody and this is all the respect you can show him. Oh, Daddy, Daddy, come back to me." She flung herself on her broomstick and sobbed to bring down the street.

"Look out," said Jack, "now for it. Shut your trap, will you, Sarah. Shoutin' there for all the street to hear."

"All the street shall hear, look 'ere. I'll tell everybody what you done. You wicked, bad man. Oh, my poor father's poor china. Swansea china, Tommy, and where is it?"

"How should I know, Sarah? Be quiet now, girl, they're coming from chapel, gel, they'll hear you. Take it easy now."

"Take it easy, you take it easy. You haven't heard nothing yet. Oh, Daddy, Daddy, where are you?"

"In his grave, thank God."

"Well I wish I was there with 'im, that's the truth."

"No bloody fear you don't, worse luck. Catch you in the same house as him as soon as you was old enough to get out, leave alone the same grave. And w'en was he promoted to Daddy, Daddy? When 'e was in Cilhendre the best thing you ever called him was that old bugger."

"Well 'e's dead and in his grave now isn't he? And don't change the subject, you. Where's his china? What 'ave you done with it? Who've you sold it to, or 'ave you given it to your fancy tart?"

"Will you shut up?"

"No."

"All right, I'm off. Come on Tommy, let's go to your house."

The two men turned. Tommy bewildered and Jack swaggering too bravely. But when their backs were turned Sarah took her broom and, running after them, brought the head of the broom down time after time on Jack's big shoulders. Dust flew in clouds, swearing choked the air. Tommy coughed to burst and the neighbours struggled for the best positions at their front windows. The men ran to cover and left Sarah victorious in the street. She looked up and down for any other challengers, but when none appeared, she stalked back into her own witch house and banged her front door.

"What 'ave you done, mun, Jack? W'at's the hullabaloo for?"

"Christ, I didn't think she'd find out so soon, mun. Old Joe Salt left her a tea set, see, when he died. In the corner cupboard it was and Sarah knew it was old because it used to be her grannie's. She brought it home and showed it to the doctor and he said it was Swansea china and worth a lot of money. I sold a cup and saucer see, to have something on the Grand National, and she didn't notice. So last Tuesday I took the sugar basin on the quiet, mun. How the 'ell was I to know she'd go and clean the bloody cupboard? She hasn't touched it in years. Daddy, my arse, Daddy – old Joe Salt – remember 'im? Christ!"

"So that's where you were on Tuesday night. Commercial traveller is it? – and me givin' you a alibi so careful. Damn, you're not more afraid of Sarah than 'spector, are you?"

"Tommy bach, you don't know the half. I'd face a regiment of 'spectors before one Sarah. I never raise my hand to 'er, though. If I once started, look out, I'd scrag her, indeed to God. I'm afraid to start. I still got a bob or two left of the china money, let's go for a couple of halves. She'll 'ave boiled dry w'en we get back."

That evening D.J. sat alone in the quiet kitchen. He, too, was feeling released and relaxed. Glad to be quiet, to be alone, to be able to think to himself. He sat in his chair, his face expressionless, his fingers tapping on the arm of the chair. When his mother came in after watering her flowers, she thought he was worrying too much and missing his friend, but she didn't speak. Her presence was for him part of the silence. Though his face looked remote and calm, he was excited and bubbling within; his poem was working out. His stomach was tensed, his fingers pulsating, the music was ordered and the words were coming right. He got up suddenly from his chair and reached for his pen and writing pad. The poem was coming. It would be all right.

"Earthbound and slothful, barely venturing forth . . ."

Honno Classics

The classics of Anglo-Welsh writing by women

Honno Classics is an imprint bringing books in English by women writers from Wales, long since out of print, to a new generation of readers.

These highly valued and respected books are reprinted with introductions by leading critics and academics in the field of English literature in Wales.

Welsh Women's Poetry 1460-2001: An anthology
Edited by Katie Gramich and Catherine Brennan.
The definitive anthology of Welsh women's poetry from 1460 to the present day. Poetry originally written in Welsh appears in Welsh and in English translation.
£12.99 ISBN 1870206541

View Across the Valley: short stories by women from Wales 1850-1950
Edited by Jane Aaron, including stories by Allen Raine, Dorothy Edwards, Hilda Vaughan, Brenda Chamberlain, Margiad Evans and others.
£7.95 ISBN 1870206355

Iron and Gold
by Hilda Vaughan
with an introduction by
Jane Aaron
£8.99 ISBN 1 870206 50 9

Queen of the Rushes
by Allen Raine
with an introduction by
Katie Gramich
£7.95 ISBN 1 870206 29 0

The Small Mine
by Menna Gallie
with an introduction by
Jane Aaron
£8.99 ISBN 1 870206 38 X
– reprinting January 2004

The Rebecca Rioter
by Amy Dillwyn
with an introduction by
Katie Gramich
£8.99 ISBN 1 807206 43 6
– reprinting January 2004

ABOUT HONNO

Honno Welsh Women's Press was set up in 1986 by a group of women who felt strongly that women in Wales needed wider opportunities to see their writing in print and to become involved in the publishing process. Our aim is to publish books by, and for, women of Wales, and our brief encompasses fiction, poetry, children's books, autobiographical writing and reprints of classic titles in English and Welsh.

Honno is registered as a community co-operative and so far we have raised capital by selling shares at £5 a time to over 350 interested women all over the world. Any profit we make goes towards the cost of future publications. We hope that many more women will be able to help us in this way. Shareholders' liability is limited to the amount invested, and each shareholder, regardless of the number of shares held, will have her say in the company and a vote at the AGM. To buy shares or to receive further information about forthcoming publications, please write to Honno:

'Ailsa Craig'
Heol y Cawl
Dinas Powys
Bro Morgannwg
CF64 4AH.